HELLO,

I MUST BE GOING

Dyan Sheldon

WALKER
BOOKS

First published in Great Britain 2018 by Walker Books Ltd

87 Vauxhall Walk, London SE11 5HJ

2 4 6 8 10 9 7 5 3 1

Text © 2018 Dyan Sheldon
Cover illustration © 2018 Anna Morrison

The right of Dyan Sheldon to be identified as author of this
work has been asserted by her in accordance with the
Copyright, Designs and Patents Act 1988

This book has been typeset in Berkeley OldStyle

Printed and bound by CPI Group (UK) Ltd, Croydon CR0 4YY

British Library Cataloguing in Publication Data:
a catalogue record for this book is
available from the British Library

ISBN 978-1-4063-6304-3

www.walker.co.uk

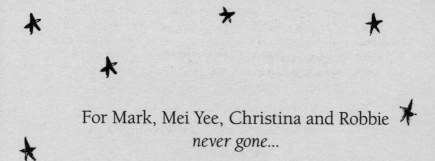

For Mark, Mei Yee, Christina and Robbie
never gone...

1

Goodbye, Hello

~

June

This is a day straight out of an advertisement for the glories of early Summer. Blue sky, whipped white clouds, big yellow sun, lush green trees and singing birds. The air is heady with the smells of flowers and new-mown lawns. Full of warmth and promise, it is a perfect day for a birthday party or a wedding. But the figures who pick their way over that freshly cut grass, under that blue sky and big yellow sun are here for neither. They are here for a funeral, for final farewells.

Sorrel Groober was a fairly normal teenage girl, not an iconic, much-loved celebrity or world leader. She was a very attractive teenage girl (and most people in Beaconspoint are aware that they've opened a paper or magazine at some time and seen her face smiling back at them), but she was only a teenage girl – loved by a few and unknown to most. Dead too soon to make a difference to the world at large. None the less, there has been such an outpouring of sorrow and grief over Sorrel's unexpected death that if Beaconspoint were a person and not a village it would be dressed all in black and keening in a dark corner, the floor covered with used tissues. There was a long, fulsome piece about her in the local paper that brought tears to many eyes. At the site of the accident a pyramid of flowers and small stuffed animals has been tied to a tree with coloured ribbons. Online, a memorial page has been set up with photos and messages. There are pictures of Sorrel when she was younger. Pictures of Sorrel that appeared in advertisements. Pictures of her on the beach and in snow and on sidewalks. Sorrel on school trips, at games, in the mall. Except for one of her crying when she was four and fell off a swing, in all of these pictures she is either smiling or laughing. A happy girl, beautiful and blessed. The messages say how full of life she was, how much she'll be missed, how she'll never be forgotten.

Almost everyone with any connection to Sorrel or her family seems to be at the graveside. Friends, relatives, neighbours, teachers. Maybe even a few people who didn't know the Groobers at all, who heard about the accident and came out of human interest. Human interest or its less attractive brother, maudlin curiosity. There is an undercurrent of murmurs – the same sighs and whispers that have been circling the town since it heard that Sorrel

Groober had been hit by a car the night of storm Bob. *So tragic … so heart-breaking … so senseless … so sad … so sorry for the parents … at least she didn't suffer … she's in a better place … we can't understand the ways of the Lord…*

Among the many mourners here today are Sorrel's three closest friends: Celeste Redwing, the best friend Sorrel ever had (and ever will have, as things have turned out), Orlando Gwinnet and Ruben Rossi.

Sorrel had missed most of first grade and was the eldest of the four. Three short weeks ago they were celebrating her eighteenth birthday. They had drifted apart some since December, but that night they were tight again, and everything was the way it had been. Meryl Groober ordered takeaway, Celeste baked a cake and Sorrel's father opened a bottle of champagne. Sorrel and her mother had a fight about something (which means it could have been about almost anything) while they were getting the glasses. Meryl stormed off to her room, leaving them all pretending that nothing had happened, so it was Orson Groober who brought out the cake with its twenty flickering pink candles, while Celeste, on her guitar, led them all in "Happy Birthday", to which she'd added original lyrics appropriate to the occasion. Sorrel's father took pictures of them on Celeste's phone. Celeste, strumming; all of them singing; Sorrel blowing out the candles;

and, finally, the four of them scrunched together, leaning into each other like meerkats, Celeste in the middle with Sorrel's head against hers, Ruben and Orlando on either side. He didn't have to tell them to smile, they already were. There was a lot of laughter that night. And now here they are, burying Sorrel under a relentless sun – and there are no smiles or laughter to be had.

Orlando and Ruben, who are acting as pall-bearers, stand on the nearby road, waiting for the hearse to arrive.

Orlando stares out at the army of headstones in front of him, keeping his back to the group gathered around the grave. It seems like most of the school is here. Even Cati Grear and her clique have turned up, as well as every boy Sorrel ever went out with (enough of them for a game of basketball), a number that includes Orlando. But all he sees when he looks at them is the absence of Sorrel – as if her image had been cut from the photograph. Orlando kicks a stone across the road and wishes the hearse would arrive. This is the last thing he thought he'd be doing this Summer, and he wants to get it over with. After the birthday party, he figured everything was back to normal between them, that the four of them would be hanging out together all the time like they used to. A slight breeze stirs the leaves, and Orlando sighs. Wrong again.

Only inches away from Orlando, Ruben faces the

mourners. He sees them as a painting, noticing the way the light falls on the dark figures, the shades of green in the leaves, the shades of expression on their faces. Sadness, of course, but also fear and relief – fear that this could happen to anyone, to them – fear that it will – relief that it hasn't happened yet. Ruben watches the gestures, the phones held high, the faces that forget not to smile. He's aware of the low hum of voices, but the only voice he hears clearly belongs to Sorrel. He hears her the night of her birthday celebration saying, "I'm eighteen! Can you believe it? Eighteen! Now I can do what I want!" Ruben closes his eyes for a few seconds. Life has a way of changing your plans, and doesn't he know it? Life and death.

Standing not with Orlando and Ruben but with the large gaggle of students from the high school is Celeste. She was both relieved and hurt not to be asked to carry the coffin. She would have said no – how could she bear Sorrel to her grave without throwing herself in after her? But she should have been asked. Was she overlooked because she's a girl? Or because Sorrel's mother doesn't have to pretend to like her any more? Determined not to think the worst, Celeste opts for the first reason. Meryl Groober has very strong opinions on what girls should and shouldn't do.

Celeste may appear to be with the group, but she's

very much alone. Around her, schoolmates tap on their phones, take selfies and whisper to one another, but Celeste will never need a snapshot to remind her of this day, and has nothing to say to anyone but herself. For most of those gathered here Sorrel Groober's is just another death – but that isn't what it is for Celeste. For Celeste it feels like the end of the world. She wouldn't have come today, but her mother, who stands on the other side of the hole in the ground in a huddle of adults, said it would look funny if she didn't. Celeste wanted to wear the red dress Sorrel always said she looks great in, the one Sorrel had convinced her to buy, but her mother said she had to wear black. What would people think if she didn't come, if she wore a bright colour? Celeste looks at the gathering, wondering what they're thinking now. She wasn't expecting such a large turnout. Sorrel preferred quality to quantity when it came to friends. In fact, most of the group surrounding Celeste were friendly with Sorrel, not friends; some probably never said anything more to her than "Hi" as they passed in the hallway – if they'd said that much. Some of them didn't even like her, or were jealous of her, or would bad-mouth her every chance they got. Sorrel would have had plenty to say about them being here. Hypocrites. Phoneys. But Celeste, who is definitely to be counted as one of the peacemakers blessed by Jesus, doesn't think any of that matters. Not any more. Even Cati Grear, who wouldn't have said anything nice about Sorrel if you'd paid her, came up to Celeste, her eyes shining with tears, to say what an awful shock it was. To Celeste what matters is that they're all here. Nobody forced them; they came because they wanted to come. Because they wished they'd known Sorrel better and because they wished they'd liked her more. Because they wished they'd been nicer to her when they had the chance – and who doesn't wish that?

The hearse appears at the top of the road. The murmur of voices becomes even softer as the pall-bearers step forward to lift out the casket. Celeste watches Ruben and Orlando, stationed behind Sorrel's twin brothers, walking as if to the beat of a slow drum. It's odd to see them in suits and ties, looking so serious and grown-up. But not, of course, as odd as knowing that Sorrel is in the pink, gold-trimmed coffin and will never be grown-up. Celeste takes deep breaths to keep herself from bursting into tears. If she digs her nails into her hands any harder, they'll bleed.

The family takes its place by the grave. Mrs and Mr Groober standing close together for a change, the twins positioning themselves on either side of their parents like bookends, the two of them wearing identical suits, identical sunglasses and identical solemn expressions. Meryl Groober, looking as if her face has been standing in the rain for a very long time and continuing to weep silently, leans against Orson, his expression less solemn than frozen.

Celeste can't watch the coffin being lowered into the ground – not without breaking down – and turns her eyes to the sky. The fat clouds remind her of pictures she's seen of Heaven. With no effort at all, she can imagine Sorrel sitting up there with the angels, smiling down on her as if to say that everything is okay. Despite her name, if this were any other day, Celeste would say that she doesn't believe in Heaven, but this is not any other day. Today, believing that Sorrel is perched on a cloud, happy and safe and alive (even if she isn't alive in Beaconspoint), is a comforting thought.

As the ceremony finally ends, almost everyone is wiping away a few tears – even those who liked Sorrel the least.

The one person who isn't – who hasn't shed a single tear since the accident – doesn't sit on a cloud, looking down on her grieving family, friends and acquaintances with an angelic smile, but stands several yards away, unseen and unsought, watching them all with a thoughtful, if sour, expression on her face. Sorrel never shared

Celeste's pacific nature.

Sorrel sees Celeste cross the grass to where Orlando and Ruben wait for her. They don't speak, but each boy reaches out for one of Celeste's hands. It is only now that Sorrel's expression changes.

The dead don't cry. But that doesn't mean that they might not like to.

2

Death Is Not the End

Lilah Redwing borrowed her company's people carrier (usually reserved for potential buyers and For Sale or To Let signs) to hold Celeste and her friends and any of their parents who needed a ride to Sorrel's funeral. Now, as they leave the cemetery, she glances into the rear-view mirror and says to the two boys in the back seat, "It's such a shame your folks couldn't make it." As if she doesn't know that Ruben's father is dead, and that both his and Orlando's mothers have been to one too many funerals in their lives to attend another if it isn't strictly obligatory. "It was such a lovely service."

Celeste, sitting beside her mother, keeps her eyes on her phone, but Ruben and Orlando, who have been staring out of their respective windows, both look at the mirror.

"Yeah, well, you know," says Orlando. "My dad had to work."

"My mom is sorry, but these things are hard for her," says Ruben.

Lilah Redwing, however, isn't a woman easily distracted from her own thoughts, or burdened by the necessity of listening to anyone else. "Really lovely. The speakers. The music. The flowers. Everything was perfect. And such a touching tribute to dear Sorrel." She sounds so moved and so sincere you'd assume that she'd liked her daughter's best friend – though in this moment, of course, fresh from the graveside, she probably thinks that she did. Lilah smiles at the car ahead of them. "I do think Sorrel would be pleased." Lilah glances over at Celeste, sitting beside her with her head bent over her phone, concentrating so hard she might be defusing a bomb. "Don't you think so, darling?" Darling, who would rather be almost anywhere than on her way to the Groobers' – a place she has never been or wanted to be without Sorrel – and who is trying not to show it, doesn't look up, but nods. "It was so upbeat and young." Like Sorrel, who now will be young for ever. "I felt it was very positive – very life-affirming."

Ruben and Orlando had gone back to watching the passing streets, each of them thinking about the slow walk to the grave, the weight of the casket, how brightly the sun shone. At this statement, which makes where they've just been sound less like a funeral than a musical, they turn to each other and exchange a look. The only thing the funeral affirmed for them was death.

Orlando's eyes are wide open, but he doesn't see the charms hanging from the mirror or the back of Lilah Redwing's head or the road in front of them. He sees Sorrel as she lay in the funeral home, wearing a dress intended for a prom, her blonde head on the pink pillow as if she was asleep. She looked so much like a fairy-tale princess waiting to be woken by the prince's kiss that he was almost tempted to lean down and put his lips on hers. Which is why, instead of ignoring Celeste's mother, as he knows he should (as they usually do), Orlando says, "You mean positive for a funeral, right, Mrs Redwing?"

Looking into the rear-view mirror, Lilah gives him the saint-like smile that is one of her specialities – that and the smile of a martyr. "You may not realize it, Orlando, but death is not the end. That's why it's important not to dwell on our temporary separation from the departed. On personal feelings. After all, it's the body that ceases to exist, not the spirit. It's only final if you're not looking at the big picture."

Orlando, of course, like most of the other mourners, wasn't looking at the big picture but at that hole in the ground. And so, although normally scrupulously polite and respectful to adults, he now says, "You mean not the end in the sense that we come from stardust and return to it?"

Celeste lowers her head even further; Ruben turns to him again, looking wary.

"No, that's not what I mean," says Lilah. "I mean that it's a beginning of the next phase. A continuation. It's just another state of being. There's the before you're born. The after you're born. And then there's the after you've lived. They're all part of the whole. Part of the circle. Sorrel may not be here, but she isn't gone. She's just stepped into a different room."

Orlando opens his mouth to point out that the room Sorrel's stepped into is six feet under the ground, but before he can get the words out Ruben kicks him in the shin.

"And it was such a good showing," Lilah Redwing sails on. "So many sympathizers. That's important when something like this happens. People can feel pretty alone. Isolated. They need to know that they aren't. That others understand and empathize." The miniature dreamcatcher and the small Celtic cross that hang from the mirror sway as they take a turn. "But even so, her poor parents. Imagine. Such a terrible thing. And the guilt they must feel. I mean, the grief, that goes without saying, but, on top of that, the guilt. No matter what. The guilt must be overwhelming."

"Guilt?" It's the "No matter what" that finally makes Celeste raise her head. Her mother has a talent for implying things she won't come out and say. And for saying one thing when she actually means something else. (Lilah has been known, for example, to suggest that some people might think Celeste had put on weight, or that some people might think Celeste could do more to help her mother, or that some people might think Celeste spent too much time with her best friend and was too influenced by her. But if Celeste confronted her mother about saying those things, Lilah would immediately deny it. "I never said that," she would say – and, of course, she never had...) "Why should they feel guilty?" Celeste goes on. "They weren't driving the car."

"No one said they were, darling. But they're parents. What parents wouldn't blame themselves? I mean, we all know it wasn't anything they did or didn't do. These things happen."

Ruben, who has personal experience of these things that can happen, leans forward. "Accidents," he says. "Accidents happen. Sorrel getting run over like that had nothing to do with the Groobers. Or even the driver. She's a victim, too. It was a bad night and Sorrel stepped into the road for some reason. That's the whole story."

Lilah blesses him with one of her beatific smiles. "Yes,

of course it was an accident, Ruben. I'm not suggesting…"
The dreamcatcher and the cross both sway non-committally. "But parents have an enormous responsibility. And Sorrel was out in that terrible storm at all hours. They have to blame themselves for that. They must think they should have stopped her from leaving the house."

Celeste keeps her eyes on the phone that she's gripping like a lifeline. And doesn't allow herself to think about who else might be to blame. "Sorrel was always walking in the rain." In the rain, no one can see your tears.

"People walk in showers, darling. That rain was more like a monsoon. But she was a very wilful girl, wasn't she?" Lilah Redwing sighs. "Headstrong. Probably they did tell her not to go but she went anyway." A second sigh joins the first. "At least they can console themselves with knowing that even if they'd locked all the doors she'd probably have gone out a window."

No one answers. All three of her passengers are looking at their phones, and thinking how they wouldn't mind going out a window themselves right now.

Lilah Redwing, however, is also not a woman who needs any encouragement to talk. "But even so, they'll feel guilty. Especially Meryl. A mother always thinks everything's her fault." Which is an interesting opinion from a woman who thinks that nothing is her fault. "And

Meryl looks like hell. Orson looks awful, too, but he's not a handsome man at the best of times, is he? And he is so much older. Meryl is ravaged. You can really see her age. Everybody thinks so. I mean, that's what you'd expect, but my heart went out to her. God knows, we all have our crosses to bear, but what she must be going through… I bet she hasn't slept even a wink since it happened. Not a single wink…"

And so they drive on to the Groobers' house, Celeste's mother continuing to talk about the funeral and the death and how Sorrel's parents must be feeling and how tragic it all is and how difficult Sorrel was and how Celeste must be glad she didn't wear anything garish and how much food will be left over since everybody's bringing something and nobody's going to feel like eating. While she talks, Celeste, Ruben and Orlando think their own thoughts about Sorrel and say nothing.

"Here we are!" announces Lilah when at last they come to a stop.

There are already so many people at the Groobers' that their voices carry into the street. Lilah has to park at the end of the block.

When they reach the house, set back from the road on an uninspired rectangle of lawn, Lilah changes from concerned neighbour to professional estate agent and pauses at the bottom of the front path to assess the property. Wondering how much it cost; if they'll want something smaller now.

Because Lilah stops and looks up at the house, the others stop and look up, too.

Something moves in the left-hand window of Sorrel's bedroom.

Lilah Redwing, who is trying to gauge the number of rooms and their likely dimensions, doesn't notice.

Orlando, who doesn't want to be reminded of the one time he was in Sorrel's room, looks away quickly and doesn't notice.

Celeste, the memory of all the times she has seen Sorrel standing at her window, watching for her, ready to smile and wave, looks, instead, at the weathervane in the shape of a ship on the roof.

It is only Ruben who looks right at the window of Sorrel's room. And so it is only Ruben who sees what could almost be mistaken for a figure, standing there, gazing out at them, waving. But Ruben is a painter, he knows about light – knows that it's only the way it's reflecting off the surface of the glass that he sees – and turns away.

Sorrel thought Celeste would look up at her window, as she always did. And would see Sorrel watching out for her, as she always did. The last person she expected to find herself waving at is Ruben, who wouldn't know which room was hers. But she continues to wave and smile, nonetheless.

Death has made her more adaptable than she used to be.

3

Now You See Her, Now You Don't

"I'm fine, Dad, really." Celeste, headset on, stands at the living-room window, watching the road. Her father rang unexpectedly. Besides his birthday and Christmas visits (when Tylor and "that man" have to stay in a hotel, and only her father is allowed to come near the house), Tylor is allowed weekly phone calls on the landline at a designated time when Lilah's at home. Lilah doesn't know that, urged on by Sorrel, Celeste has been texting and talking to her father on her phone in secret for years. These calls, of course, are usually planned in advance. Which is why Celeste is watching the road; her mother is due back soon. "I'm doing good."

"So you keep saying," says Tylor, "but I'm still worried about you. So is Jake. A death like this isn't something you get over in a couple of days."

"There's nothing to worry about. I promise. I really am good."

Celeste blames herself for the accident. She was meant to go to a party with Sorrel that Sunday night, but Lilah wanted her to spend the evening with her. Celeste was always doing something with Sorrel. How about a little quality time with her parent for a change? After all, Celeste would always have another friend, but she'd never have another mother. Celeste couldn't say no. And so Celeste bailed on Sorrel and stayed home and watched a series about remodelling houses with Lilah. Sorrel stayed home and had a fight with her mother, and then walked into a car.

"I still think you should spend the Summer with me and Jake," says her father. "I'm sure the change would do you good. Get you away from all the things that remind you of Sorrel."

"You know I'd like to." She'd love to. There are no memories of Sorrel in Brooklyn. "But I really can't. I have a Summer job—"

"You could have a Summer job with us. You could help out in the shop. And the band has some gigs coming up. You could join in. It could only help to have a pretty young girl with us. People get tired of looking at balding old farts."

"I'm really sorry," says Celeste, "but I just can't."

"Is this because of your mother?"

Of course it is. Lilah has made it clear that visiting Tylor and "that man" is not in the script. Astra, says Lilah, is far too young and sensitive to be put through that, and if Astra can't go, then Celeste can't either. Fair is fair. If Celeste defied her mother and spent the Summer with Tylor, Lilah would take it as a betrayal. Choosing her father over her mother. Siding with the enemy. Celeste might as well stab Lilah in the heart, and then stand on her cold, dead body and play her guitar.

"You know how busy Mom is in the Summer," says Celeste. "She can't really deal with the house and Astra and everything else by herself."

"I'm sure they could survive for a few weeks without you. Astra's nearly fourteen. She doesn't need a babysitter any more."

That's what he thinks.

"It's complicated, Dad. Astra can be a little flaky sometimes. You know."

In fact, Tylor doesn't know, because no one has told him, about all the things Astra loses, or all the times Astra has forgotten to turn off the stove, or lock the front door, or even come home.

"Well, what about coming for a long weekend, then? Just a few days. Surely your mother could manage on her own for just a few days."

As if she knows they're talking about her, Lilah's car pulls into the driveway.

Celeste steps slightly to one side, making her presence at the window less noticeable to anyone on the drive. "I have to go."

"Just say you'll think about it," says her father. "Sleep on it."

"I…" The car doors open. Lilah gets out from the front, and Astra and her best friend Winnie climb out of the back, and go round to the boot. Astra and Winnie have been swimming, and stand together, lifting out their bags and towels. Celeste's heart stumbles. Sorrel is standing behind her sister and Winnie, looking right at her. "I have to go." She looks down for a second, to end the call, and when she looks up her mother and the girls are coming up the front path, but there is no one else by the car.

Of course not, thinks Celeste. *I was seeing things.*

And doesn't know if that is a good thing or not.

4

The Light Gets Up
to More Tricks

There was a time when, if he suddenly thought of Sorrel Groober, Ruben saw her as he once painted her for an art project – "Girl Out of Water". The four of them had gone kayaking on the lake one afternoon and were just about to head in when a dog fell out of a passing boat. Sorrel saw it before anyone else, and jumped in to rescue it. Ruben took a photo when they got back on shore, Sorrel sopping and laughing, still holding the terrier in her arms. Usually Sorrel never forgot she was a model and always looked ready to have her picture taken; never so much as a single hair out of place. But after she jumped in the lake her hair was a mess, her make-up was ruined and her clothes looked like she'd worn them before quite a lot. She looked fantastic. It was the best photo he'd ever seen of her, which is why he turned it into a painting. He gave Sorrel "Girl Out of Water" for her birthday. She was really excited about turning eighteen, being an adult. "Now you're so old," Ruben joked, "you can start collecting art." It wasn't among the scores of pictures of her that had been placed all around the Groobers' living room the day of the funeral. Maybe her mother threw it out. When they dropped Sorrel back home the day she jumped in the lake, her mother had a fit when she saw her. You'd think she'd come back covered in tattoos and piercings, not just wet and dishevelled, the way Meryl Groober had carried on. Or maybe the painting was in Sorrel's room. Either way, Ruben wasn't about to investigate further. Mr and Mrs Groober were in the middle of the crush of guests, shoulder to shoulder and looking, with their grim faces, as if they'd stepped out of Grant Wood's painting "American Gothic" – or were about to step into it.

That, however, was then, and this is now. Now when he suddenly thinks of Sorrel what Ruben sees is the flickering light by the office door in the laundrette, and the broken clock on the wall beside it that always says it's seven twenty-eight. The washing machine at home can no longer be repaired, but Ruben's mother refuses to replace it. "That's just one less thing to worry about," she said – smiling as if having a washing machine is something that causes everyone sleepless nights. And so, on the day Celeste called him to tell him Sorrel was dead, Ruben was sitting in the launderette, reading a book about Vincent Van Gogh that he found in a garage sale. Celeste was sorry for bothering him, and wanted to know where he was, if he was busy. When he told her, she asked him to stop by on his way home. She wasn't crying and she didn't sound upset, but he could tell immediately that something was wrong. Only he had to go straight home when the laundry was done; his mother would be anxious if he was late. Celeste said she figured she should tell him herself, because his mom doesn't answer the phone when she's working so no one would have given her the news. And Ruben said, "Tell me what?" He stared straight ahead while she told him, straight ahead at the flickering light and the broken clock.

Which is exactly what Ruben is staring at now, sitting in the same chair in the same launderette. If he were still painting, which he isn't, he would do a portrait of that flickering light and that broken clock: "The Day that Time Stood Still". Because that's what it feels like this afternoon, that he is in the same day – same moment – when he got the call from Celeste. Except, of course, that today he isn't reading about Vincent Van Gogh but thinking of Sorrel Groober. How well he knew her – he and Orlando had been friends with her and Celeste since their freshman year, hanging out at school, hanging out after school, a little gang of four. How little he knew her – he knows her favourite colour, her favourite food and her favourite band, but he doesn't know what she was afraid of, what stopped her from sleeping, if she believed in God.

Ruben looks up to see that his wash is done. He gets to his feet, goes over to the machine by the window, and opens the door. *What was Sorrel thinking as she stepped into the road that night?* he wonders as he starts throwing the wet wash into his basket. *Was there half a nanosecond when she saw the car coming? Was she frightened? Did she scream? Or did she never know what hit her?* He straightens up, glancing to his left as something catches his eye.

A face is gazing through the window at him. She isn't wearing make-up and her hair is in two plaits, so that she looks about twelve, but it's Sorrel's face. Sorrel's face, with that break-your-heart smile. So close that if there weren't a sheet of glass between them he could reach out and touch her. The basket of clothes drops from Ruben's hands. When he's retrieved it and looks out of the window again there is no one there.

Of course there isn't, thinks Ruben. *It was the light throwing images.* It was probably his own reflection that he saw. After all, a vivid imagination runs in Ruben's family. That and insanity.

It doesn't occur to him that the dead know how to use light to their advantage.

5

Too Much Time in the Sun

If Orlando ignores the matter of Sorrel's death (*if* he can), the Summer should be pretty good. He's lifeguard at the private lake, which is a cushy job with minimum work and maximum pay. Since it isn't an ocean he doesn't have to worry about killer waves and undertows. Which means there isn't really much to do besides stay awake. Mainly, he has to keep an eye out for kamikaze toddlers whose mothers are looking at their phones and not at them. Besides that, he teaches a beginners' swimming lesson every morning, depending on interest, and occasionally rescues someone in a boat who lost their oars or whose motor died. But the best part of the job is that most of the lake people are older couples or families with young children so he rarely runs into anyone who knows him. He's just the lifeguard, what's-his-name. There's nobody asking him about Sorrel or telling him how sorry they are. It'll be different when school starts again. Then there will be sympathy and curiosity; the looks and the whispers. Then he'll go back to being Orlando Gwinnet, popular student and high-school hero. Orlando's always been sought after socially (especially by girls), but it wasn't until Sorrel dumped him that he let himself be lured by all the attention. Parties. Cycling weekends. Dates with girls he had no interest in. Lots of dates. Did Sorrel even notice? He has no idea. If she did, he's sure she didn't care. He was busy, she was busy. They were all busy. What he does know is that none of it made him feel any better about the break-up. Popularity isn't all that it's cracked up to be.

Today he had the afternoon shift. He pedals slowly, taking the scenic route, in no hurry to get home. Maybe no one talks to him about Sorrel at work, but that doesn't stop him thinking about her. Orlando thinks about her a lot.

He was the last of the friends to find out about the accident. Plugged into his iPod, he was doing his evening run and had just passed the barn that is all that remains of the old Inkman farm – the halfway mark – when he felt his phone vibrate. Because everyone knows he runs at the same times every day of the year – holidays included and weather no obstacle – he checked to see who it was. It was his father. His father isn't a man to waste anything, even a phone call; it had to be important – even more important than merely making sure that Orlando was where he was supposed to be. And it was more important. "Sit down," ordered his father. "I have to tell you something." Bernard Gwinnet isn't just economical with phone calls; he is a man who gets straight to the point without apologies or tears. And he's very good at breaking bad news in a bloodless, official way. As a county policeman, Officer Gwinnet (which is what Orlando calls his father – but only privately, of course; to his face he calls him Dad or, sometimes, sir, though he's careful never to sound facetious) gets plenty of practice. Orlando, used to doing as he's told, sat down. *Late last night… Raining like the devil… Walked into the road… Hit by a car… Pronounced dead at the scene…* "That can't be true," said Orlando when his father was done doling out the facts. He could see Sorrel laughing as she cut her eighteenth-birthday cake. How could she be dead? His father said it was absolutely true. "You all right?" he asked Orlando. Which proved how true it was. After they hung up, Orlando stayed down at the side of the road, his headset dangling around his neck, the music still playing but very far away – in another world, another life – seeing the single wild flower growing beside him, wondering what it was. He doesn't know how long he sat there, thinking of Sorrel, remembering… He kept trying to imagine what had happened. To picture it. How could she just step into the road without looking? How could she not have seen the lights of the oncoming car? Why hadn't he called her last night and asked her to hang out? He could have done that. He'd been keeping his distance for months, but after her birthday he'd promised himself that he'd do stuff like that again. Make things like they used to be. Okay, so she dumped him, but they were still friends. They were friends a hell of a lot longer than they were a couple. She'd put her arms around him the night of her party; she even kissed him on the cheek. He was sure she would have come over, if he'd asked. They could have watched a film, or played cards. Instead he sat in his room watching a thriller he may have seen before and listening to the rain while Sorrel walked in front of a Ford. Orlando's mind travelled over the same small track like a toy train, round and round and round, going nowhere and never arriving. You don't expect your friends to die. Not when you're in your teens. Even Orlando, the sole survivor of four children, wasn't expecting that. Two of his brothers died before they were born and the eldest, Raylan, was unlucky. Unlucky or careless, depending on how you looked at it. Orlando might have sat there all night if a cop car hadn't stopped to see if there was something wrong. The officer knew his father and recognized Orlando, of course. The policeman drove him home.

He coasts down Spoon Hollow Hill, picking up speed, imagining a starless, rainy night, imagining a car suddenly coming around that bend up ahead; wondering what Sorrel's last words were, her last thought. And then, as he leans into the bend, he sees her standing at the side of the road, almost in the trees, watching him pass like a spectator at a race. He glances back over his shoulder, but there is no one there.

That's what happens when you sit out in the sun all day, thinks Orlando. *You start seeing things.*

But he can't help wondering if the dead see things, too.

6

Things that I Miss About You

~

July

It wasn't until the next afternoon that Celeste found out about Sorrel's accident. She had just arrived home from her Summer job at the day camp and was doing the dishes left from breakfast when her phone rang. She'd been texting Sorrel whenever she had a minute to herself, and thought it must be her answering. At last. But, of course, it wasn't Sorrel. "Hi, darling," said Lilah. "I just had a phone call from Professor Groober." And burst into tears.

Celeste stopped what she was doing and sat down. All the while her mother struggled to tell her what had happened, Celeste listened patiently, staring at the plastic bag caught in the branches of the oak tree in the back yard. Plastic lasts for ever. Celeste didn't cry. "It can't be true," she said when Lilah finished. "She just had her birthday." Which made her mother start sobbing again. Celeste advised her to take some Rescue Remedy and camomile tea to help her calm down. After she hung up, Celeste finished the dishes, and then called Ruben because she knew his mother never answers the phone so no one would have told her and Ruben wouldn't know what had happened. After that she went to her room, picked up her guitar and started writing a song. The song is called "Things That I Miss About You". She's been working on it ever since, adding verses and taking them out. It's a long list. But no matter how many changes she makes, it always ends with the same line: *The thing I miss most is you.*

It is a rainy afternoon. Celeste is sitting on her bed, working on the song now, singing softly, when the door opens and her mother pokes her smiling head in.

"Hello, darling." Lilah steps into the room. "What are you doing?"

Another girl – Sorrel, for instance – would say something sarcastic. *Whipping up a soufflé. Building a bridge. Deconstructing the works of Harold Pinter.* But Lilah doesn't take kindly to sarcasm; it reminds her of Celeste's father. "Nothing," says Celeste. "Just messing around."

Her mother's smile steps up a notch. "I'm a little worried that you're spending a lot of time in your room by yourself lately." She gives the guitar the sort of look that is usually reserved for dung beetles. "Playing music." Tylor Redwing plays music, which makes it something to be discouraged. "I really don't think that's healthy. It's so internal. You need to see people. Get out more."

Celeste leans against her guitar. "I go to work all week, Mom. That's getting out, and it's full of people."

Her mother shuts the door behind her. "You know what I mean. You need to socialize. See your friends. When I was your age, Summer vacation was the time for the beach and parties and just hanging out. For having fun."

Of course, when she was Celeste's age, she hadn't just buried the best friend she'd ever have.

Celeste absent-mindedly plucks a string. "I just don't feel like it right now."

Lilah sits down on the foot of the bed, smoothing the spread with one hand. "Oh, honey, I know you're upset about Sorrel – this has upset us all – but I thought we agreed not to dwell on it. The best thing to do with something unpleasant is to put it behind us and move on. You can't spend your Summer moping around." Moping, in Lilah Redwing's world, is any mood that isn't positive and agreeable – and is a serious crime. Celeste's father moped a lot.

"I'm not moping, Mom. And I'm not upset. I just like to take it easy on the weekend." She smiles like a girl who never mopes and isn't upset. "Anyway, everybody has jobs or else they're away. There's not much going on."

"Really?"

"Yes, really."

"Well, that's good news. I'd hate to think you were missing out." She pats Celeste's knee. "It's just that everyone always noticed how preoccupied you always were with Sorrel. I tho— This is your chance to do different things. To hang out with the people you've been neglecting – maybe even make some new friends."

"I have plenty of friends. I don't need any new ones."

"What about your old friends, then?" You don't get to be estate agent of the year three years in a row by giving up easily. "Why don't you ring Orlando? You haven't seen him since…" She pats Celeste's knee again. "I'm sure he'd be glad to have your company." If Lilah's smile goes up many more notches, she'll blind them both. "Everyone thought when he broke up with Sorrel—"

"Mom, please." Her mother has been pushing Celeste to date since middle school – which was when Lilah herself started dating; after that she was rarely without a boyfriend. Ironically, when Celeste and Sorrel first became friends, Lilah encouraged the friendship, thinking that Sorrel's looks would attract the boys and that Celeste would get a boyfriend from among Sorrel's rejects. But it didn't quite work out the way she had hoped. Now Lilah would be happy to see Celeste with almost anyone except Ruben. Not only is he artistic (Lilah knows from

Tylor Redwing just how unreliable those artistic types can be), but he also has the added disadvantage of being too short for a girl of Celeste's height. Orlando, however – handsome, super jock, school star, tall – has always been her boy of choice. "Orlando's not interested in me and I'm not interested in him."

"I wasn't suggesting…" Lilah's smile is now mildly affronted. "All I meant was that you've been friends since you were little. Good friends. Remember that Halloween you sprained your ankle because your father made you that crayon costume you couldn't see in and you fell off the Roebucks' porch and Orlando carried you all the way home?"

Celeste sets the guitar down beside her on the bed. "Mom—"

"I can still see the two of you coming up the road. This tall skinny rabbit with this big blue crayon wrapped around his back. I should've taken a picture. But your father—"

Having moved past moping and Sorrel as topics of conversation, Lilah will sit here for the next hour, finding more and more things to blame on Tylor Redwing if Celeste doesn't stop her. "Mom!" Celeste gets to her feet. "You're totally right. I haven't seen Orlando since the funeral. I should check in on him. I think he took it pretty hard."

"Now that's more like it." At last her mother looks pleased.

Celeste is not so pleased. Her conversation with Lilah has upset her. As far as her mother is concerned, the period of Celeste's mourning ended the day after the funeral if not immediately after the burial, but for Celeste it has barely begun. She has no intention of checking in on Orlando; right now all she wants is to get out of the house and away from her mother before she says something they both regret. She grabs her raincoat and an umbrella, and, cheerfully calling out, "See you later, Mom," walks through the front door – resisting the temptation to slam it behind her, the way Sorrel would have done.

Sorrel rang Celeste only minutes before the car hit her, but Celeste never got the call; not then. Her phone had gone missing. As it does. Astra is always picking it up by mistake and then leaving it wherever she happens to be when she figures out it isn't hers. It wasn't until the next morning that Celeste found her phone under a pile of her sister's things on the sofa – and heard Sorrel's teary, hysterical message. *Cel? Where are you? Pick up! Please! I have to see you. I'm coming over. I finally told Meryl the truth. She went ballistic. We had the biggest fight.* And hears it now. *Cel? Where are you? Pick up! Please! I have to see you.*

I'm coming over. I finally told Meryl the truth. She went ballistic. We had the biggest fight. Cel? Where are you? Pick up! Please! I have to see you. I'm coming over. I finally told Meryl the truth. She went ballistic. We had the biggest fight…

What if Astra hadn't misplaced Celeste's phone? What if Celeste had answered? *Calm down,* she'd have told Sorrel. *I'll meet you halfway.* Then Sorrel would have come over; then Sorrel would still be alive. Instead of being dead. Celeste constantly has to remind herself of this. *Dead. Dead. Dead.* She still finds herself thinking, *I'll call Sorrel now* or, *I have to tell Sorrel that,* and reaching for her phone. Even though she knows there is no Sorrel on the other end. Which doesn't mean she hasn't tried. In the first few days after the accident, Celeste called Sorrel every day, but of course her phone didn't exist anymore, either; like Sorrel, it had been crushed under the wheels of a Ford. Celeste wonders what she would have done if the phone hadn't been destroyed; would she have left a message on voicemail? Would she have waited for a reply?

Sorrel's death is the worst thing that has ever happened to Celeste. Worse than primary school when she was bullied for being so quiet. Worse than when her father left them and her mother fell apart. Worse than when the other kids started making fun of her and calling her Shrek in middle school. Worse than when Astra went from being a difficult child to a really difficult teenager. Worse than when her father moved to Brooklyn. Worse than when he married Jake and her mother banned him from ever stepping foot in her house again. Worse than every bad, humiliating or painful experience Celeste has ever had – all put together and intensified a thousand times. And there have been plenty of them.

Not that anyone would know how devastated Celeste is. It might be different if she'd had to go straight back to school and face everybody – all that sympathy mixed with stories and speculation – but the Summer is protecting her from the brunt of that, and by the time the Summer's over Sorrel's death will be in the past. No, despite her mother's concern about moping – and her obvious desire that Celeste put Sorrel so far behind her that she as good as never existed – Celeste is presenting her usual cheerful, upbeat self to the world at large. At work she deals with the daily crises of the day camp – the squabbles, the mishaps, the minor injuries – with competence and good humour, smiling and laughing as if she doesn't have a care in the world. At home she deals with the daily crises of her mother and her sister – the things lost or forgotten, the panics, the moods – with efficiency and enough patience to stock a troop of saints. Sorrel's name is rarely mentioned – not at work, of course, but not at home either. When Celeste does run into someone she knows, she agrees about how awful what happened to Sorrel was, and quickly changes the subject.

Only Tylor seems to suspect the truth. "You have to let it out," he tells her every time they speak. "Keep working on Sorrel's song. The song'll help." And every time they speak he asks if she's sure she's okay. It's not too late to change her mind and come down for the rest of the Summer. "Of course I'm okay," Celeste repeats again and again. "Life goes on." And she goes on, acting as if her heart doesn't feel the way a gutted building in a bombed-out city looks.

Between her Summer job and helping her mother, Celeste has a lot to do, and, as everyone will tell you, busy hands keep the mind busy, too. By being more efficient, more responsible and busier than ever, Celeste manages not to think about Sorrel or that night or that Sorrel was coming to see her or why. Celeste manages not to think of these things most of the time. Or a lot of the time. Or some of the time. And when she does think about Sorrel she tries to picture Sorrel in Heaven – or someplace like Heaven – and happy. Celeste believes that she and Sorrel will meet again. Though, at the moment, she doesn't foresee that happening for quite a while.

Right now, however, as Celeste flees her home, Sorrel is

the only thing she's thinking about. Memories of her play like a video in her head. Sorrel talking. Sorrel laughing. Sorrel dancing. Sorrel putting on make-up. Sorrel singing off-key. Celeste stops under a large oak tree, and takes out her phone, flicking through the photos from a few weeks and a few lifetimes ago at the birthday celebration, until she finds the one she wants. And there they all are, smiling as if nothing bad has ever happened to any of them, and never could. And there's Sorrel with her head on Celeste's shoulder. Celeste stares at the screen, feeling Sorrel leaning against her. Although she has no memory of having felt it at the time, she also feels Sorrel's breath on her cheek. It takes a few seconds for her to get her own breathing back to normal and turn off her phone. *She's in Heaven … she's happy…* Celeste tells herself. *Mom's right, death isn't the end…*

As it happens, only two of those statements are true.

Fighting back tears, Celeste looks around her in some confusion; she doesn't know where she is and has no idea how she got here. In front of her is a large and unfamiliar yellow house with white window frames, shutters and doors, and a veranda that stretches from one side to the other. It is, in fact, a lot like the Groobers' house, but larger. As her eyes fall on the house, Celeste gives a yelp of alarm and drops her phone. Sorrel, it seems, is not in Heaven. She does, however, look pretty happy. She's sitting on an old-fashioned rocking chair, wearing an equally old-fashioned yellow fisherman's mac and matching sou'wester hat, and eating an enormous piece of chocolate cake. There's chocolate frosting all over her face.

Celeste retrieves her phone, telling herself not to be stupid. There may be a girl on that porch, but she can't be Sorrel. Sorrel is in the pink box, six feet under the ground. Or, as Lilah Redwing would say, no longer in this dimension. Celeste blames the rain, she's not seeing clearly because of the rain. That's why Sorrel had her accident, because of the rain. And because she was crying. Neither she nor the driver could see properly. Poor visibility. Not paying enough attention. The distortion of looking through water. Anyway, look at how the girl is dressed. Sorrel would never wear a coat and hat like that. They're as chic as green wellies. And she never ate cake, especially chocolate (cake is fattening and chocolate made Sorrel break out).

Nonetheless, since she is staring at the girl and doesn't want to be impolite, Celeste waves. Tentatively. The girl, busy chewing, doesn't wave back. Of course she doesn't. Sorrel would wave back, she'd be overjoyed to see Celeste, but this girl isn't Sorrel and has no idea who Celeste is. Crazy girl, waving at her in the rain. Celeste steps out from under the tree, and squints through the veil of rain. The girl really does look like Sorrel, even with frosting all over her face. Celeste sniffs. The scent of lilacs, Sorrel's scent, is in the air. How is that possible? Lilacs don't bloom at this time of year. Is it a sensory memory? Or does it mean that it really could be Sorrel sitting on the porch, moving back and forth in the creaking old rocker? What if it is?

"Sorrel?" she calls. "Sorrel, is that you?"

This time the girl looks right at her, and smiles. "Hey, Cel! How's it going?"

If a heart could dance, Celeste's would be doing the fandango.

"Sorrel! I wasn't sure it was you. I've never seen you dressed like that before."

"You've never seen me dead before, either."

"I can't believe it's really you!" Celeste is not the sort of girl to troop over other people's property uninvited, but this is a unique situation. She leaves the road and strides across the lawn, only stopping when she reaches the porch. "Sorrel. What are you doing here?"

"Eating chocolate cake." She stuffs the last piece into her mouth. "You know how Meryl would never let me have anything like that. I mean, God forbid I should put on an ounce or get a pimple. That would be my life over." Sorrel puts the empty plate down on the floor beside her.

"But now it is. So I'm making up for all the cake I never had."

For the first time in quite a few days, Celeste laughs. "I'm so glad to see you. I didn't think. I…"

"Isn't this wild?" Sorrel opens her arms to embrace the air. "It's raining. And you still have that same yellow umbrella! Just like when we first met. Remember?"

And how could Celeste forget? It was a Saturday in their last year of middle school. Celeste had walked into town under her yellow umbrella to post a birthday present to her father without her mother knowing and was on her way home. Sending Tylor secret birthday gifts were then the only times she went against her mother's wishes (even if they are unspoken wishes) and Celeste was feeling guilty. Her mother would have been so hurt if she knew.

"Of course I remember. You were sitting under a tree in the rain." Sorrel had moved to Beaconspoint during the Summer vacation, but, although Celeste knew her by sight (who didn't?), they'd never spoken. "Crying." In public – right there in front of the whole block of houses and passing cars.

"Anybody else would've kept on walking," says Sorrel. "I mean, who but you would just accost some stranger sitting on the ground sobbing her heart out?"

"I felt bad for you. I wanted to help." If she were a place and not a person, Celeste would be a sanctuary. Celeste can't bear to see anything in distress, whether it's an insect or a human being. She's been bitten trying to rescue a cat, has broken her wrist trying to rescue a spider and got a black eye (accidentally) trying to rescue a drunk from the middle of the road. She always wants to help, and feels bad about everything.

"That's your MO all right," says Sorrel. "Celeste saves the world. You should either be a superhero or a registered charity."

"I was worried about you. You looked really unhappy."

"I was really unhappy." She grins. "You remember what you said to me? You said, 'I'm sorry. I don't want to bother you. But are you okay?'"

Celeste remembers it as if it happened only minutes ago. "You said you were fine."

Sorrel winks. "You said I didn't look fine. In case I hadn't noticed, you told me I was crying, my nose was running and I looked like I had two black eyes."

"You really looked awful," laughs Celeste. "Then you said the raccoon look was totally in that year."

"And you sat down next to me and said, 'Oh that's what it is. I thought you were upset about something'. That cracked me up."

Sorrel had had a big fight with her mother – another big fight, although Celeste didn't know that then, didn't know how often they fought – on top of all the stress of moving to a new home and a new school and having to make new friends. Which was why she was sitting there, crying in the rain. Celeste, already something of an expert on the subject of stress, totally understood. She thought Sorrel would have to be superhuman not to get stressed.

"And you said, 'My God, you haven't even met my mother yet.'"

They wound up laughing in the rain, much as they are laughing in the rain right now. That first time, though, the laughter didn't end with a front door suddenly opening and a woman with a grim set to her mouth stepping out.

Celeste freezes, staring at the new figure on the porch the way a deer will stare at oncoming headlamps. The woman doesn't smile, or give any indication that she can or ever would smile. "Can I help you?" She points the phone in her hand at Celeste. "Is there something you wanted?"

Celeste has never felt threatened by a smartphone before. But, of course, she has never trespassed before, either. She blinks. "Oh, no. I'm sorry. I – I was just—"

"This is private property, you know."

"I know. I mean, I'm sorry. I—" *I what? I was talking*

to my dead friend? Celeste starts walking backwards. "I'm going. I didn't mean— I'm really, really sorry if I bothered you."

She looks over to the rocker, hoping for a little moral support, but Sorrel has already gone.

It isn't just the tough who get going when the going gets tough.

7

There Isn't Enough Natural Light in the Bookshop for It to Be Up to Its Old Tricks

Although the Rossi house is real, and sits on a real street among other real houses, in a very real town, the Rossis themselves live in what almost could be called a parallel world. Especially Sylvia, of course – she is a permanent resident – but when he's at home Ruben lives there, too. A dark world where science and reason are abandoned on the threshold and where sorcery and magic can work miracles; a world populated by people who don't actually exist.

When he's not at home, Ruben does live in the real world, and in that world he has a Summer job working five days a week in Curiosity Books, Beaconspoint's independent bookshop. Ruben started working here because of his mother. Sylvia Rossi writes fantasy fiction under the pseudonym of Gaia Pendragon, and is relatively successful. Last Summer, when she was still leaving the house, Ruben accompanied her to a signing at the shop.

(HERE TODAY! THE AUTHOR OF THE BESTSELLING MOONDANCER SERIES!) Mr Goldblatt, the owner, was so impressed by Ruben (he organized the signing, handmade the phantasmagorical posters and knows a lot more about fantasy fiction than Mr Goldblatt) that he offered him a part-time job on the spot. Ruben took the offer because it gives him money, keeps him occupied and, haven of fiction that it is, makes his mother seem normal – or, at the very least, more normal.

Sundays are pretty quiet in the shop and, because there have been only three customers all morning, Ruben has spent most of the day making a display for the children's window. He drew elaborately detailed pictures of a spaceship, a plane, a sailboat, a camel, a horse, an elephant, a hot-air balloon and a magic carpet – each with at least one person on board – and cut them out to place among the books. Then he painted a sign to go with them: SUMMER FUN – READ YOUR WAY THROUGH SPACE AND TIME AND DIMENSIONS AND AROUND THE WORLD. Right now he is straightening the books on the tables, making sure they're in the right stacks. He works almost robotically, not really paying much attention to the novels and biographies and cookbooks as he straightens and moves them into the right piles – until he picks up a book that is on the wrong table and finds himself staring at a picture of a girl looking through a window. The window is in a house, not a launderette, and the girl (who is dark, not fair) is looking out, not in, but Ruben immediately travels through space, time and dimensions, and is standing unloading the washing machine in Spin and Rinse. Seeing Sorrel staring back at him. Clear as day. And, despite the striking differences between the cover illustration and what he imagined he saw, the memory it triggers is vivid enough that he drops the book on the floor so quickly you'd think the dark-haired girl had waved at him. He retrieves it immediately, wiping it off on his jeans and replacing it precisely. He goes back to the desk as the phone starts to ring. Saved by the bell. At least for the time being.

Those two weird incidents – at the Groobers after the funeral and in Spin and Rinse – lasted only a few seconds, and Ruben has tried very hard to forget them. He didn't think it would be difficult to do in all the other seconds in his life – like losing a grain of sand on a beach – but they don't want to stay gone. Like bad luck, they keep returning, sneaking up on him when he's least expecting it. Making him lose track of what he's doing, where he is. He was shaving in front of the mirror over the kitchen sink when suddenly he imagined he saw Sorrel smiling back at him; he was lucky not to slice off his chin. He was handing a receipt to a man in a straw hat and red-framed glasses when he thought he saw Sorrel's face in the lenses and more or less threw the slip at the customer. He was gazing in the window of the computer shop, thinking about electricity, when a blonde head suddenly appeared beside his reflection, smiling, and he turned so fast he nearly knocked over Lily-Rose Masuki (who, except for the hair, doesn't look anything like Sorrel Groober).

And now this. All he has to do is look at an indifferent illustration and he's in the launderette holding a basket of wet washing and staring into Sorrel Groober's smile.

Is this happening because he had such a crush on Sorrel, is that why? Ruben straightens the stack of bookmarks next to the register. He calls it a crush, but it was almost an obsession. Even in those last six months, when he pulled away from them all and saw her less and less, even then he thought about her all the time – in an if-only sort of way. Or is this happening because he really is beginning to lose his mind?

The clouds scuddle in after noon, bringing with them the rain. Business picks up. Grateful to be busy, Ruben helps find titles, answers questions, orders books that aren't in stock and rings up sales. He is busy enough to have no time to think – or to imagine.

At the end of the day, Ruben straightens the shelves

and displays again, and cashes out. Then he systematical-
ly goes around the shop turning out the lights, but stops
abruptly when he reaches the reading section at the back,
where there are chairs and a small sofa. There's a boy in
scruffy jeans, a faded plaid shirt and an old baseball cap
sitting cross-legged on the sofa, bent over a book. Where
did he come from? How could Ruben have missed him?
Ruben starts to say that it's closing time but gets no further
than "Excuse me, but—" when the boy raises his head.

"Can you believe it?" says the boy. "I never even
thought of reading one of these before." And holds up the
book in his hands, *Dark Worlds Old and New* (Book Four
in Gaia Pendragon's Moondancer series). "It's really good.
Severely. I was gripped from the first paragraph. She has
a terrific imagination. Not like most people. You know
what I mean. Most people can't imagine anything they
don't already know. Don't you think that's true?" The boy
shakes his head. "So how come you never said how good
your mom's books are?"

The boy, of course, is not a boy, but Sorrel Groober.

Except for when she fell in the lake, Ruben's never
seen Sorrel dressed in anything that wasn't just washed
and ironed and glaringly female. When she wore jeans
they weren't jeans that were meant to get dirty, and
they'd been ironed. He looks behind him, but whether

he's looking to make sure that there's no one there, or because he hopes that there is, that this is some sort of joke – one of those TV programmes where they trick you into showing the world what a dope you are – he doesn't know. But there is no one there. He knew that there wouldn't be. He's all alone with a dead girl who's reading one of his mother's books. There are way worse situations to be in, he knows that, but right now he can't think of any. He opens his mouth to say something – *what? why?* – but nothing comes out.

Sorrel, however, was always a talker, and death has done nothing to diminish her conversational skills. "It's funny, isn't it? I know your mom and I've seen her books around, but I never even picked one up. God knows why. I guess I thought I'd get around to it. You figure there's always tomorrow, but then – surprise! – there isn't. You never had tomorrow, you only had today." She rolls her eyes. "But look who I'm talking to. You know all about that, don't you?"

Ruben stares at the section of books in front of him – Current Events – and says nothing. He knows a lot more about that than he'd like to know.

"But, seriously," says Sorrel. "How come you kept it so quiet? If my mom could write like this I'd've told everybody I knew, and everybody I didn't know too. I mean, hey, this sure as hell beats nagging, arguing and complaining. Which are pretty much my mother's major skills."

By concentrating very hard, Ruben manages to get his heartbeat back to normal and find his voice. "We're closing. I'm turning out the lights." He is calm, matter-of-fact – as if he's talking to someone who's actually there. "You can't stay here. You have to go."

"But I'm really enjoying the book. I don't want to stop reading now."

"This isn't a library," says Ruben. "You have to go."

She tilts her head, almost as if she's flirting with him. In which case, she really waited too long. "Why? Who's going to know if I sit here all night? Who're you going to tell?"

He'll know, that's who will know. It'll drive him crazy. Crazier. But she's right, of course, there's no one he could or would tell.

"I'm turning out the lights," repeats Ruben. "You can't read in the dark."

Sorrel grins. "You don't think?"

He's being ridiculous. Is he being ridiculous? Yes, he's out-of-the-galaxy ridiculous. *Can't stay here. Can't read in the dark.* For God's sake, she isn't real. She's not a trick of the light this time, because there isn't much light, but she is a figment of his imagination. The imagination he clearly inherited from Sylvia Rossi. Sorrel's death must have upset him even more than he'd thought. That's what this is. He's more upset than he thought.

"You're right," he says. "Why shouldn't you stay. Knock yourself out. Read anything you want. Read everything in the shop. Make yourself at home." And he snaps out the last light at the back and strides away.

He gets his things from the desk and picks up the keys, but as he reaches the front door he sees Sorrel standing looking in through the children's window, his mother's novel tucked under her arm.

She waves, and he has to stop himself from waving back.

8

You Can Run but You
Never Can Hide

For a change, as Orlando lies in bed watching the night bleed away, it isn't Sorrel who is on his mind, as she often is these days. Orlando had a dream. He and Ruben were having lunch, sitting at their usual table in the school cafeteria. Orlando had a thick sandwich and a bowl of salad in front of him, but Ruben had a plate of homemade lasagne that looked and smelled just like the lasagne Ruben's mother always made. Orlando couldn't figure out how that was possible. Nobody makes lasagne like Ruben's mom. And then he looked over at the kitchen and saw Sylvia Rossi working behind the counter. He waved, but she was too busy to wave back. He turned to ask Ruben when his mother decided to become a dinner lady, but Ruben was deep in conversation. He was talking to the person next to him about painting: depth and movement, light and shadow. It's been a long time since he heard Ruben talk like that, and he was passionate and intense – the way he used to be. The only problem was that there was no one there. "Ruben! Ruben!" Orlando had to kick him to get his attention. "Ruben, man, who are you talking to? Are you talking to yourself?" Apparently, he was talking to Sorrel. "Sorrel's dead," said Orlando. "Don't you remember? Don't you remember the funeral? You can't be talking to her." Ruben said that dead isn't the same as gone. She was right there, right beside him. Why couldn't Orlando see her? She was clear as the food on the table. He and Sorrel hung out together all the time now, he said. "Don't ruin it for us," ordered Ruben. "Stay out of it. We're having a good time."

The alarm goes off, and Orlando slowly gets out of bed, still thinking about Sylvia Rossi's lasagne and Ruben talking to Sorrel. He doesn't need a dream interpreter to know what this one was about. He dreamed that Ruben's mother was working in the cafeteria because he hasn't seen her since before Christmas, when Ruben started acting weird. Since Ruben's father died, Orlando didn't spend as much time at the Rossis' as he used to – none of them did – but all of a sudden he wasn't spending any time at all there; Ruben wouldn't even let him in the house. No more lasagne suppers, no more hanging out till all hours, no more crashing on the fold-out. Whenever Orlando stopped by to pick up Ruben, he'd be on the porch before Orlando turned up the front path. The reason for the Sorrel part of the dream is obvious, too. It's because he thought he saw her that time, standing at the side of the road. He didn't see her, he knows that, but every now and then he gets an instant replay of that moment, and wonders what it was he did see. Obviously, what his brain's done is conflate these two things – his worry about Ruben because of how odd he's been acting all year – and his unease about himself, seeing things that aren't there.

Orlando puts on his running clothes, and silently leaves the house. Beyond any doubt, Orlando's twice-daily runs are the best part of his day. This is one of the ways he gets rid of tension; this is one of the times he feels most like himself. Out of the house and away from his father's expectations, completely alone with just his own thoughts and no one talking to him or wanting him to talk to them or needing anything from him or seeing him as a sports legend in the making. The morning run is his favourite, out at first light when almost no one else is stirring yet. He always chooses a route where the houses are few and far between, so that it is just him and the road, the sky and the trees, and, on this morning, a pale wash of sunlight and the smell of roses in the air. Because it's so early, no cars pass him and the houses still have their eyes closed. Usually he listens to music while he runs, but today he's turned it off and the only sounds are the occasional call of a bird, rustlings in the woods and underbrush, and his own feet slapping against the ground.

A plane flies overhead, a bird calls and Orlando's footsteps thud against the asphalt, steady as a heartbeat. The further he goes, the more the dream recedes. His breathing is measured, his back wet with sweat as he turns onto Brandywine. It's a long, narrow lane with a creek running on one side and a hill rising up on the other. There are only four houses on the entire stretch, three of them up steep drives and out of sight, the fourth across the creek and guarded by a wall of pines. A chipmunk scoots across the road, a kingfisher whistles thinly over by the water, a deer steps delicately through the trees. As if Orlando is the only person in a perfect world. He rounds the bend, and the world quickly becomes just a little less perfect as another runner comes up beside him. Without turning his head, Orlando can see purple shorts and hairless legs. She must have come out of the woods on the left. Silently. Orlando slows down, expecting her to pass him. When she doesn't, Orlando picks up speed. To his surprise, his unwanted companion keeps pace. It's only then that he realizes that, besides the roses, he smells lilacs.

In the same instant that his heart jumps a beat she says, "So what'd you think of the funeral? Was that a farce or what?"

This can't be happening. He knows that. There is no evidence to support the existence of ghosts. None. Nada. Zilch. Ghosts are all about light. Lights and shadows. Reflections. Electricity. Optical illusions. Maybe he should add bad dreams to that list.

"I mean, seriously?" Sorrel glides along beside him as if she's on wheels. The girl who always said that running was for giraffes. "My closest two hundred friends? What a joke." Now he looks over. She's wearing a top to match the shorts and her favourite earrings – chains of gold stars – that gently swing as she moves. Her hair is pulled back in a ponytail. *Ponytails are for children*, was another thing she always said. He can hear himself breathe, but he can't hear her breathe. Her voice, however, is loud and clear. Instead of stopping, he goes even faster. "God, what hypocrites people are. Did you catch Cati Grear and her coven? You must've. Like a murder of crows around a stranded fish. And crying like they didn't hate my guts and always made sure I knew it. Thank God for waterproof mascara, right? Where would the world be without it?" She shakes her head. "It's weird, isn't it? People either pretend to like you when you're alive, or they pretend to like you when you die. You'd think they could come up with one policy, and stick to it."

Maybe he's still dreaming. That has to be it. He hasn't woken up yet. He thought he woke up, but he didn't. It's one of those dreams. On and on and on. He's still back in bed, still sleeping, but his dream has moved on from Sylvia Rossi making lasagne in the cafeteria and Ruben telling him not to ruin things for him and Sorrel, and now he's dreaming that he's running and she's beside him, critiquing her own funeral. "I'm dreaming," he gasps. "There's no one else here. It's just a dream."

"And what about all those guys?" Sorrel is not gasping; Sorrel might as well be sitting down. "Every boy I ever went out with was there. It was like a Who's Who of losers. Except you, of course." She laughs. "You're not one of the losers. You're my friend. You I liked. But the rest of them? God help me, even that jerk Shoehorn was there. I mean, seriously? After the way he bad-mouthed me because I broke up with him? Give me a break."

"I know that this is a dream," says Orlando – not to her – there's no way he's talking to a hallucination – but to the road ahead of him. "All I have to do is wake up."

"And let's not forget that stupid dress they buried me in. I looked like I was going to a dance, not a grave. And that coffin. Chrissake! What was I supposed to be? Barbie in a box?"

Orlando digs his nails into his palms. *Wake up! Wake up! Wake up!*

"You can accuse my family of a lot of things. My dad's

useless. My mom's a menace. The twins are oblivious. I mean, if no one told my brothers I was dead they probably would never have noticed, they're always so stoned. And if Meryl the Peril thinks she could fool me with all her tears and acting like her world just ended, she's wrong. Believe me, she was sobbing from guilt, not sorrow. But you know the one thing you can't accuse them of? Do you, Orlando?"

Wake up! Wake up! Wake up! Wake up! Orlando forces himself forward with one last burst of speed.

Sorrel is right beside him, giving no sign that her lungs are about to burst. "No one could ever accuse my family of good taste, that's what!" she shouts.

A horn sounds behind him. Orlando finally stops running and jumps to the shoulder, just managing not to fall over. He bends forward, his hands on his knees, trying to catch his breath. It's a minute before he realizes that Sorrel is gone.

He doesn't let himself wonder if she'll be coming back.

9

A New and Different Shopping Experience

Celeste knows she'll see Sorrel again. There is no way Sorrel would appear just once – twice if you count the time Celeste thought she saw her in the driveway with Astra and Winnie – and then abandon her. But who knows how hard it is for her to visit? If ghosts could just come and go as they please between dimensions, they'd be everywhere. Conquistadors in Disney World. Pilgrims in the supermarket. British soldiers marching across football fields and tennis courts. Whole tribes of women, men and children walking the highways, wondering what happened to all the trees. There is also the fact that Sorrel never had a very good sense of direction – she could get lost just going around the block; how lost can she get moving in space and time? Of course, there is the small matter of ever finding Celeste alone to factor in as well. She shares a room with Astra and is surrounded by people all day at work and by her family all night – everybody wanting her attention – and keeping her busy. What Celeste needs is space.

"What do you mean you don't feel like coming?" Celeste's mother can smile and look hurt at the same time. "You love the mall." The keys she's holding jangle unhappily. "My God, Celeste, if you and Sorrel spent any more time there they would've given you your own bench."

This is a slight exaggeration, of course, but it is true that Celeste and Sorrel loved hanging out at the mall. They would spend whole days there just talking and being together, buying nothing but a coffee or a diet soda, roaming through the wings and levels as hunter-gatherers once roamed the plains – rather than at either of their homes, where they always felt watched. But Celeste has never loved going to the mall with her mother and sister. In their separate ways, they manage to make it as much fun as having your teeth scaled. Astra has to try on everything she sees, Lilah buys her everything she wants, and Celeste usually ends up carrying the bags. Not that she would ever say she hates shopping with her family. Not to them, anyway.

"I just don't feel like it today." Celeste never has the house to herself. Peace and privacy at last. She wants to make it easy for Sorrel to find her. Sorrel has to know how to get to Celeste's house, no matter how many dimensions she has to cross to manage it.

"Don't be silly," coaxes her mother. "It's ages since you bought anything new. Why don't I treat you to something special? How about a Summer dress?" Lilah doesn't think that Celeste wears enough dresses. Celeste may not have her sister's looks, but she doesn't help herself any, doesn't make enough of an effort. "Something to catch the boys' eyes."

"I don't really need a new dress." Or want to catch the boys' eyes. "I work with little kids. I'm better off in dungarees."

"You can't wear dungarees to a party." Lilah Redwing fits the world to her, not herself to the world. She is not a woman who is easily defeated. "Or if you have a date. I heard they're having dances down at the lake every weekend till September. Isn't that where Orlando's working?" She sighs. "I really thought that after he broke up with Sorrel—"

Celeste cuts her off. "Anyway, I have a new song I've been writing. I was going to work on that."

"A new song." As if Celeste said she plans to spend the day counting blades of grass. Lilah considers songwriting a waste of time.

"It's about oceanic pollution," explains Celeste. "It's called 'Walking on Water'."

Lilah might be smiling at a two-year-old who believes

Father Christmas is going to turn her into a real princess. "I'm sure it's lovely, darling, but writing a song is not living. You haven't gone shopping since Sorrel passed away. Don't you think it's about time?"

"This has nothing to do with Sorrel." They went to the mall right before Sorrel's birthday. They bought balloons. "I'd just rather stay home and chill, that's all."

"Darling. We've been over this before." Now her mother's smile is worried, but it is not worry that contains much sympathy or patience. "You can't shut yourself away all Summer. Life goes on. You have to get back on the horse. Sorrel would want you to."

As if Lilah has any idea what Sorrel would want. She'd be horrified if she did.

"I'm fine, Mom. I'm on the horse. Really. It just doesn't want to go to the mall today, that's all."

Lilah puts on an innocent, pleading voice. "Not even for *me*?"

There are times when it almost seems as if Celeste is the adult and her mother the child. Celeste, as the adult, can't say no. It would be like throwing a bucket of water on a purring kitten.

Celeste sits in the back seat as they drive to the mall, her eyes on the passing scenery – though she's paying so little attention she probably wouldn't notice a herd of zebras galloping by. Astra sits in the front next to their mother, head bent over her phone. Winnie is in Orlando at the moment, and Astra (who would give anything to go somewhere so cool instead of being stuck in boring Beaconspoint all Summer) is counting the days till she returns. If she weren't able to message Winnie constantly she would probably die. Lilah does all the talking.

She thinks she's about to clinch the deal on the Westov house on Cedar Ridge. She thinks she's going to go on that weekend retreat with her friends in the Autumn. She thinks that Celeste is going to be very glad she came along today. A change is as good as a rest. And if you ask her (which no one did) Celeste could use both. After all, what is life but change (asks the woman who has greeted the most major change in her life so far with relentless rage)? That's why Lilah is encouraging Celeste to get out more and see people. You're only young once. And then you're not young and you have nothing but responsibilities and obligations and a hundred things to do. Lilah knows how close Celeste was to Sorrel, of course she was. But it isn't as if Lilah doesn't know what it's like to lose a part of your life. Divorce may not be the same as death, but she went through hell when Tylor left her, absolute hell. She didn't think she'd ever recover. But look at her now. She has scores of new friends. She's had dates with some terrific, responsible, serious men. Her career is thriving, and she has more interests than ever before. Celeste will recover, too, in time. It's just that Lilah worries that Celeste isn't seeing Sorrel clearly now that she's passed. Grief can make you idealize the departed. (Something that anger, clearly, doesn't do.) Make you forget the things about them that weren't so great. But Sorrel wasn't perfect, was she? Not that Lilah's saying anything against poor Sorrel – of course she isn't – she's just saying that she had her faults like everyone does. Lilah thinks that after they do some shopping they should have lunch in that French bistro place, the one with the chequered tablecloths? Won't that be fun? She's sure they must do hamburgers – Astra's unlikely to eat anything else on the menu. Celeste watches two Jack Russells pull a woman along the pavement, and wishes she'd stayed home.

Astra and Lilah get out of the car as soon as they park, but Celeste stays buckled in, staring out at the concrete sprawl and the colours of the automobiles gleaming in the sun, seeing herself and Sorrel, arms linked, laughing as they crossed the car park, the golden star balloons for Sorrel's birthday bobbing above their heads. This is too weird without her. What was she thinking? Why couldn't she simply say no? "Maybe I'll just wait for you here."

"You'll do no such thing." Her mother yanks open the

back door. "You're coming with us. I know Sorrel could be selfish, but she wouldn't want you to sit in the car all afternoon just because she passed away."

The three of them crawl through the mall, in one shop and out another, Astra and Lilah talking together, their conversation moving seamlessly from an outfit they wouldn't wear in prison to what they've heard about that new Summer blockbuster – Celeste trotting gamely beside them, trying not to show how much she'd rather be home writing about islands of plastic clogging the seas. Or marooned on one. In the past, if she was forced to come with them, she would text or ring Sorrel while she was parked outside the changing room, minding the bags. But not any more, of course. Between the relentless lighting, the tedium of watching her mother and sister shop and the incessant sound of their voices, by the time they reach the second level Celeste can feel a stress headache building behind her eyes.

In every shop, Astra rifles through racks and tables, pops in and out of the changing rooms so many times to get her mother's opinion that she's quickly on a first-name basis with the woman at the door. Lilah likes everything Astra picks. Cute. Adorable. That colour looks great on you. Fits like a glove. She is less enthusiastic about Celeste's choices. Everyone says short skirts make you look taller.

Everyone says bright colours are more flattering to brunettes. She read somewhere that patterns make you look wider. She's sure someone told her that stripes make you look fat. "But you're the one who's going to wear it," says Lilah. "Don't listen to me. You get what makes you happy."

Celeste takes the dress that will make her look taller, the one that won't flatter her, the one that will make her look the width of a doorway and the one that will make her look overweight into the last cubicle and pulls the curtain shut.

When she turns around, Sorrel is sitting on the narrow bench, feet up, hugging her knees. Flouting all of Lilah Redwing's fashion rules, she's wearing a red-and-blue striped top and green-and-yellow striped shorts. On her feet are black-and-white striped socks and metallic-pink high heels. The girl who was destined for the cover of *Vogue* has become the fashion equivalent of a train wreck.

"What was that crack your mother made – 'I know Sorrel could be selfish'? What's that supposed to mean?"

Celeste is relieved to see her, not surprised. She should have known Sorrel wouldn't let her come to the mall without her. "You know my mom."

"Try that one on first." Sorrel points to the pink and orange tunic. "And no, I'm not sure I do know your mom. Enlighten me."

"Yeah, you do." She pulls the tunic over her head. "She's friends with Adelita next door to your folks. Adelita told her how you and your mom were always fighting and everything. My mom disapproved. She doesn't think you showed your mom enough respect."

"That's because you're the perfect daughter. You ruin it for the rest of us."

Celeste has her first laugh of the day. "That's me. Perfect!" This is just the way it used to be, her and Sorrel in the changing room together. Making each other laugh. "What do you think?"

Sorrel tilts her head appraisingly. "It looks great. Those colours really bring out your eyes. And anyway, I always knew she didn't like me."

"She's never said that." Lilah never says anything that could be held against her in a court of law. Celeste starts taking off the pink and orange tunic. "But sometimes she'd make little comments. I think I'll try the stripes next."

"She's still making little comments." Sorrel reaches for the stripes and holds it out. "I like the way she decided Orlando dumped me."

"She likes Orlando. She can't believe any girl would dump him."

"Oh, I know she likes him. She wants you to go out with him."

"She wants me to go out with anything that breathes." Celeste gives Sorrel a sideways look.

Sorrel winks. "As long as it's a boy."

"She didn't use to be like that. At least I don't think she was. Well, maybe a little. But she's a lot worse now because of my dad. She took it really personal." Celeste frowns at herself in the mirror. "Do you think this makes me look fat?"

"Of course it doesn't," says Sorrel. "And you know what else is irritating? She keeps saying I *passed away*. I mean, seriously? She makes it sound like I moved."

"The short skirt next." Celeste wriggles out of the stripes. "My mom doesn't like negativity. She thinks saying somebody's dead sounds so final."

"It is pretty final." Sorrel hands her the skirt. "It's not like I'm in Oshkosh or LA. You can't pick up your phone and call me. Or get on a plane and visit, can you?"

"But I wish I could," says Celeste.

Sorrel says, "Me, too."

Celeste tries on the skirt and the wildly patterned dress. The skirt, says Sorrel, shows off her legs. The dress makes her look cool and funky.

"So which one do you think looks best?" asks Celeste as she gets back into her jeans.

"I think you look great in all of them."

"Really?"

"Yeah, re—" Sorrel breaks off. Beyond the curtain someone's calling Celeste. "Uh-oh," says Sorrel. "The voice of the mother is heard in the changing room."

"Celeste?" Lilah's feet appear under the curtain. "Celeste? Is that you? Did I hear you talking? Is someone in there with you?"

"No, of course not. I'm just coming. I—"

"What's taking you so long?" Her mother whips the curtain aside. "Your sister and I are starving."

Celeste glances over her shoulder. Sorrel, of course, is gone.

She's getting really good at making an exit.

10

There Are Some Things for which Aluminium Foil Is No Help at All

In some ways, Ruben's house is very like a medieval castle. Impenetrable; exclusive; visible but isolated – although there is, of course, no moat surrounding it, just a front porch and a small yard. It is an ordinary wooden two-storey built in the early twentieth century, in the middle of an ordinary suburban street made up of similar houses, not an imposing stone fortress set high on a hill. But it's no less impassable for that. There hasn't been a visitor since before Christmas.

Ruben wakes up with sunshine in his eyes and the thought in his head that Van Gogh's genius may have been the product of insanity, unsure of whether he thinks this is good news or bad. It's early yet, but Ruben gets out of bed, pulls on yesterday's jeans and T-shirt, and pads onto the landing. His bedroom, on one corner of the house, has windows on two sides and, because he never shuts the blinds, is as light as outdoors, but the landing is as dark as a stormy winter night. His mother is still up; he hears her typewriter clacking away in the room across from his.

"Mom?" He taps on the door of what used to be the spare room in the days when they had guests and is now her office – *ratatattattattattatat*, so she'll know that it's Ruben and not some imposter. "You want anything? I could fix you a snack."

"Good morning, dear!" Her voice is bright and cheerful, as if she just got up and is looking forward to the day (rather than not having been to bed at all and planning to miss the day completely). "You know what I'd love? A nice camomile tea. Help me sleep."

"Coming right up." Ruben's been Sylvia's son for a long time now; his voice, too, is cheerful and bright. Most families believe themselves to be normal no matter what evidence there is to the contrary; Ruben knows that his isn't.

Ruben descends the stairs in the dark and crosses the living room into the dining room and then to the kitchen as if the curtains are open and the lights all on. An example of practice making perfect.

The kitchen and the basement are the only places in the house where the electricity is allowed to function. In the kitchen are a refrigerator, a stove, a toaster, and the table where Ruben works on his laptop; in the basement are the boiler, the dryer and the broken washing machine. He makes a tea for his mother and a coffee for himself, and brings them both upstairs. Sylvia Rossi sits at her desk, dressed in tartan leggings, a shirt that once belonged to her husband and slippers that look like bats, working on her ancient manual typewriter. The only light in the room comes from a Coleman lantern, which leaves the corners of the room shadowy and dark.

Ruben puts the cups down on the desk and kisses her cheek.

"Thank you, sweetheart." She touches his hand. "How did you sleep?"

"Great." Which is what he always says. If he were awake all night while the hounds of Hell clawed at the door of his bedroom and bayed for his blood he'd still say he slept great. His mother generates enough anxiety and disappointment herself without Ruben adding to it. She has to believe that he's always fine. My son, the problem-free zone. "What about you, Mom? Isn't it time you got some rest?"

"I just want to finish this chapter." Sylvia Rossi (or Gaia Pendragon, as she's known to her many fans) started writing in her spare time when Ruben was little. It was Ruben's father who encouraged her to give up her job and concentrate on her writing, which turned out to be a prescient decision. If you're agoraphobic, electrophobic, paranoid and generally view the world as a hostile environment, being a writer is the perfect job. You don't have to deal with other people, go outside, open the curtains or even turn on the lights if you don't want to. You can spend most of your time all by yourself in a room where the windows are protected by space blankets, safe from the threats and dangers that lurk beyond your walls. "It only needs another paragraph. Then I'll get some sleep." She has the lifestyle of a hermit and the hours of a vampire.

He sits in the armchair next to the desk to drink his coffee while she has her tea – their morning ritual on mornings when she's still awake when he gets up – and he makes a list of the things she wants him to buy while he's out.

"So anything exciting happening at school today?"

Ruben reminds her that school hasn't started yet. It's still Summer vacation.

"Of course it is." She gestures to the sheet of paper in the machine. "I get so involved in what's going on in my novel that I forget what day it is." And sometimes what hour and what year.

When they finish their drinks Sylvia goes back to her paragraph and Ruben goes out to the car.

On Monday, one of his days off from the book-shop, Ruben drives into Peakston to the nearest market that sells organic produce, grains, dairy and meat sub-stitutes. Among the many things Ruben has researched online is food, and he's learned enough to convince himself that food that's overly processed, flooded with hormones, steeped in pesticides and packaged in plastics or aluminium can wreak havoc on the body's chemical balance – causing all sorts of things you don't want like cancer, depression and dementia. His mother's chemical balance is delicate enough as it is – it doesn't need help from outside agents to achieve havoc.

His mother is, of course, the reason Ruben worries about his sanity. What if it's hereditary? It could just be a matter of time before he's wrapping himself in foil and crawling past windows on his stomach. Not that Sylvia was always like this; she used to be just a regular mom. Went to PTA meetings, threw him birthday parties attended by other children, went shopping, had friends, worked part-time as a secretary, talked to the neighbours, turned on the lights – all the usual stuff. She gradually started to change after his father died. She didn't see her friends as often, went out less and less, wrote more and more. But there was still the veneer of normality. She slept at night and was up in the day. People came by, she went to the supermarket and the stationery store, she talked on the telephone, she cooked meals, she watched TV with him, the lights were still on. And then, last December, on the day that would have been his parents' twenty-first wedding anniversary, Ruben came home to find the living room was dark. He shouted out for her. "Mom!" He was late getting home; there should have been lights on by then, smells of cooking, the radio playing classic rock. He dropped his things on a chair and called again. "Mom! Where are you?" From where he stood he could see that the kitchen, too, was dark. He tried the nearest light switch but nothing happened. It took him a few minutes for his eyes to adjust before he realized that she'd taken every bulb from its socket and covered the windows in aluminium foil. "Mom?" There was still no answer, so he went upstairs, taking the steps two at a time. She wasn't in her bedroom or her office. He kept calling. And at last she answered. "I'm in here, honey." Feeling slightly nervous, though he wasn't sure why, Ruben opened the door to the bathroom. His mother was sitting in the tub, dressed to go out, with a helmet made of aluminium foil on her head instead of a hat. "Did you have a good day?" asked Sylvia. "I didn't hear you come in."

Of course she was still upset about his father – they both were; it hadn't been even a year, a very short time in the world of death – but he hadn't realized just how upset she was. Hadn't understood that Enzo being struck by lightning had made the whole world so threatening and unsafe for his mother that she finally had to retreat from it. Since that first afternoon, her symptoms have changed from time to time (she's come out of the bathtub, stopped wearing the helmet, replaced the foil on the windows with space blankets and no longer stays beneath window level when she crosses a room), but she hasn't got what he would call any better. Not so you'd notice. She won't use electricity (no computer, no phone, no lights – although she has never suggested shutting down the kitchen appliances or the central heating and will use his laptop, unplugged, if she wants to look up something or check her emails or for the occasional online shopping trip), but it's okay if he uses electricity so long as it's not too near her. A woman named Eliza handles her website and answers her fan mail, and Ruben handles her server account. When he has to be out of the house all day he leaves her a flask of coffee, a flask of herbal tea, a bottle of spring water and her lunch in a cool box. She'll use the landline if she has to (she only has to press one button if she needs to talk to him), and occasionally will leave the house for short periods (but only if Ruben is by her side). Sometimes she's afraid of being either brainwashed or abducted by aliens, other times she's terrified of being kidnapped or blown up by terrorists, still others it's being shot by some random psychopath or being killed by falling space debris that keeps her indoors. If she were willing to travel any distance she wouldn't take a bus, train or plane; wouldn't eat in restaurants or stay in a hotel. Which, if she were willing to travel, would limit her destination options considerably.

At first he thought this would be temporary. That it was no more than a very delayed reaction to the shock and grief. He was sure it was the anniversary that triggered it – their first without his dad – bringing the shock and horror back in full force. Ruben believed that once his mother had fully processed her feelings, once she'd completely recovered and had moved on emotionally – had accepted that special occasions no longer included Enzo and never would again – that then the space blankets would come down, the lights would go back on and things would return to how they'd been. But, of course, this has yet to happen. The only thing his mother has got over is being normal; the only thing she's settled into is her ever-changing and wide-ranging catalogue of anxieties.

Ruben doesn't want anyone to know about Sylvia. He's afraid that if it became public knowledge she would be sent away for treatment. He can't bear to think of her in some institution, lonely and frightened; can't bear to think of losing her, too.

In the happier past, the Rossis' bright red door had always been open to Ruben's friends. *Come on over ... hang out ... stay for supper ... spend the night.* When Ruben and Orlando were younger there was a tree house and camping in the backyard, picnics and barbecues, birthday parties and fireworks on the Fourth of July. When they were older and the girls joined them, there was a firepit and a finished basement with a ping-pong table, a foosball table and a TV. But then Enzo Rossi was electrocuted by Nature and all that stopped. Ruben has never discussed his mother's state of mind with anyone, not even Orlando, the brother he never had; he simply shut everyone out. His official story is that his mother is working and can't have any disturbance. "Writers," says Ruben, "they're delicate geniuses." When he and Sylvia are invited somewhere as a family – a barbecue, a party – or there's something at school parents are expected to attend, he always says his mother's away promoting her books. "Half recluse, half performer," says Ruben. The invisible woman; mother of a boy who is half liar, half magician.

It took his friends a while to realize that things were different. Orlando was the first. After his brother was killed, Orlando lived as much at the Rossis' as he did at home – possibly more. He slept on the fold-out in Ruben's room and they did their homework together at the kitchen table; he helped around the house and played Scrabble with them. It was inevitable that sooner or later he'd notice that the drawbridge was up on Castle Rossi. "What's going on, man?" Orlando asked one rainy afternoon when he called for Ruben and found him already waiting on the porch. "Do I smell or something? You never let me in the house any more." Ruben laughed (chuckled, *Really, hohoho, man, you are funny*) and mumbled something vague about his mother, work and stress. "I get that," said Orlando. "But it's not like she has to hang out with us. She doesn't even have to see me. We can go downstairs or to your room." Ruben said it was complicated. "Complicated," echoed Orlando. "Complicated like astrophysics? Or complicated like you don't want to talk about it?" Ruben said, "Both."

Ruben always enjoys the drive into Peakston. Alone and unlikely to run into anyone he knows, this is as relaxed as he gets without being knocked out. There's a programme on the radio about the national parks. Ruben's father used to talk about taking a family trip to Yellowstone one Summer. They'd get an RV and the three of them would drive across the country, stopping wherever they wanted along the way, Ruben and his father sketching the mountains, trees and skies, his mother full of songs and reading out interesting stories in local papers. Enzo saved up for years; the trip of a lifetime. But not in his lifetime, as things turned out. Ruben doesn't think about that now. The presenter's voice is soft and soothing, and, as autumn days go, this one is a five-star, top-of-the-line day. The air crisp, the sun strong, the leaves like vibrant brushstrokes of colour against the pale blue sky. It's almost as if he's on the road – he and his mother and his father – taking the trip that never got taken. He's reminded of a song his mother used to sing before the music went out of her life, something about mountains and God painting the scenery. And then he pictures Sylvia in her dark, stuffy room; decor courtesy of the Devil himself.

Ruben pulls into the car park and grabs his canvas tote bag from the passenger seat. You might imagine that thinking about his mother would cast a cloud over Ruben's morning, but he's whistling what he remembers of the song about God painting the scenery as he strolls to the market. His life is a little weird, he's not saying it isn't, but it's not that bad. Sylvia may not be the prototype of mental health, but she isn't unhappy. She feels safe on the upper floor of their house, wearing her husband's old shirts and writing her novels that take place in a faraway and much better world, where she is the heroine, his father is the hero and things always end well. But she doesn't hurt anybody; and she doesn't hurt herself, which is the important thing. He's no longer afraid of being orphaned.

Bread and Land is a small, hippie kind of store – the store that time forgot – all brick and wood and everything unpackaged. The clerk has blue hair and a tattoo; there's a small red Buddha next to the till and a sign over the chilled case: *If you're not part of the solution, you're part of the problem*. There isn't an inch of unused or wasted space in the room. Four customers at a time make it look busy; this morning there are six people inside, making it look like a mob scene. Ruben grabs a basket and shuffles through the narrow aisles. He fills paper bags with rice, beans, pasta and nuts. He's standing in front of the produce section, trying to choose between the broccoli and the cauliflower, when a voice beside him says, "Why not get both?"

It's a familiar voice, but not in a good way. More in the way that someone who flees to a remote island to escape pursuit would feel if he got off the ferry to find his stalker waiting for him, holding a piece of cardboard with his name on it. Ruben looks over. Sorrel Groober is standing beside him, juggling two stalks of broccoli and a cauliflower – one, two, three, one, two, three – seamlessly as a circus performer. He hasn't seen her since that afternoon in Curiosity, and, as the days put that incident behind him, has managed to convince himself that this absence of Sorrel would continue. That whatever had made him imagine her in the first place had passed. He should have known better. He should have known that as soon as you have a few minutes' peace something's going to ruin it. In this case a talking apparition. One dressed for a snowstorm in a heavy, hooded parka, woolly mittens and knee-high boots. Is there climate change in Heaven or has Hell finally frozen over? He should never have thought about his mother not hurting anyone and him not winding up an orphan, that's probably what put Sorrel in his head.

Another thing Ruben has researched extensively online is apparitions. Spectres for dummies. He thought it would give him some control over whatever was going on in his head. Turned out that there's a lot more information out there than he'd imagined. "Ghost sightings" got him over five million results; "hauntings" another five million plus; "ghost visitations" fifty-one million and still counting. Some of the sites and blogs are obviously bogus, the gibbering of delusional or desperate minds. But some of them are impossible to disbelieve. People see things, hear things, smell things; their pets see, hear and smell them, too. Unfortunately, the result of all this new knowledge has been not to empower him, but to make him feel that he's locked in the boot of a stranger's car and has no idea where they're going. So that now, although it's still hard for him to believe that she's really there, juggling vegetables, he does have to acknowledge that there's a chance that she is, and it's that chance that makes him hiss, "What do you think you're doing?"

"I'm helping you." One, two, three – she tosses the broccoli and cauliflower into his basket.

He glances around; no one's looking his way. "I don't want your help. Go away!"

"But you need my help." She picks up a tomato and sniffs it. "Smell that, it's gorgeous. It smells just like a tomato. My mom shops in supermarkets. The tomatoes don't smell like anything much."

"I don't need your help. Put that down."

She puts the tomato into his basket (which, technically, is putting it down), but doesn't go away. "I didn't know you did the grocery shopping. That's very evolved of you."

"You seem pretty evolved, too," whispers Ruben.

She gives him a smile that a few months ago would have been like a punch in the heart. "Where's your mom?"

"Where do you think she is? She's home."

"I'm surprised, that's all," says Sorrel. "I thought she did the shopping. She always had that box of coupons in the car. I mean, my God, your mom's like supermom.

Always baking and cooking. And remember that year my parents were in Florida for my grandmother's funeral and Sylvia invited me and the twins over for Thanksgiving? There must've been thirty people there and she made all that food and she was singing the whole time she was in the kitchen. It was awesome."

The last Thanksgiving as opposed to the first. "Thirty-eight," amends Ruben. She used to like a crowd.

"See? That's exactly what I mean. My mother? My mother thinks ordering takeaway is cooking and paying the housekeeper is cleaning. But your mom—"

"Yeah, well, today she's really busy. Working."

"Oh, that's right. She works a lot." A statement that sounds like a question. "I remember that, she was always working. She must write like a book a week."

Is she probing? She's probing. Sorrel always was the nosey one, the one who pried. Celeste pretty much believes what you tell her and Orlando respects a person's privacy. They both accepted that they didn't go to the Rossis' any more, or that, if they did, they didn't go past the front door. But not Sorrel. She was always pushing, always looking over his shoulder when he came to the door. Putting on her how-can-you-say-no-to-me smile. The smile that worked with everybody else, but not with Ruben Rossi – not any more.

"Go away, Sorrel. Now." He is firm and unyielding. Whether she's a genuine restless soul or an early sign of hereditary insanity, it can't hurt to at least act as if he's in charge. "Everybody's going to think there's something wrong with you, dressed like that in the middle of August."

And here comes the smile. "No they won't." She holds up a bunch of purple carrots. "No one can see me but you."

Is that good or bad? If they can't see her, what can they see? Can they see broccoli, cauliflower and tomatoes leaping into his basket? Carrots dancing in the air? Ruben talking to no one?

"Put those carrots down and leave." He's trying to talk without moving his lips but not with much success. Ventriloquism isn't one of his natural talents. "People are looking at me." Are they? He can't risk checking, just in case every other shopper in the store is staring at him, open-mouthed, phones in hand, fingers ready either to film him or to call the police to come and get the boy who's talking to himself and levitating vegetables. Do they think he's on drugs or just crazy? Are they afraid he may be dangerous or do they just feel sorry for him? "I mean it, Sorrel."

She makes a little-girl face and puts on a little-girl voice. "'I mean it, Sorrel,'" she mimics. "Or what, Ruben?" The carrots start swinging in an alarming way. "What are you going to do if I don't do what you say?"

This is, of course, a very good question. What can he do? He can hardly frogmarch her out the door. "Please, I'm begging you. Just go away and leave me alone."

"No," says Sorrel. "I'm not going anywhere."

"Okay. Have it your way." This may be establishing a pattern – Sorrel turns up, Sorrel won't leave, Ruben retreats – but he can't see what else he can do. He wrenches the carrots out of her hand and puts them, the tomato, the cauliflower and the broccoli back. He retraces his steps and empties the bags of rice, beans, pasta and nuts back into their bins, neatly refolding the bags and putting them back as well. And all the while he does this he is aware that not only is Sorrel watching him, but that other customers are watching him, too. The clerk leans against the counter with an amused smirk on her face. With as much dignity as he can muster, Ruben walks out of the store. Once on the pavement, he half turns, as if his attention has been caught by something up the street, but really he is looking through the window of Bread and Land. Sorrel is standing in the produce island, reaching for the onions. She winks.

It's all he can do not to wink back.

11

Belief Isn't Always Necessary

Mercifully, Officer Gwinnet has been very busy lately, which has taken some of the pressure from his son, but today Orlando gets home later than usual to find his father waiting for him. "Where've you been?" demands Bernard. "Don't you get off at three?" Orlando says he had stuff to do. "Well, better late than never," says his father. "There's still time to shoot some baskets before I have to go to work." He eyes him accusingly. "It's been a while."

A while is not necessarily long enough. "I'm kind of tired, Dad," says Orlando. "Maybe tomorrow."

"Tired? How can you be tired? You're still a boy. Your brother used to—"

His mother interrupts the catalogue of Herculean feats accomplished by Orlando's brother before her husband can get started. "Oh, Bernard," she says. "The boy's been working all day—"

"And now he gets to play, Suzanne." Her husband's word is final.

Shooting baskets is not a form of father–son bonding for Bernard Gwinnet the way it is for some men. It's training; training and making sure that Orlando isn't slacking off. To Bernard playing is all about aggression, competition and winning – three things that don't come naturally to this son. In the world of Bernard Gwinnet, as the old saying goes, nice guys don't win ball games.

They shoot for half an hour. Orlando darts and weaves and hurls the ball at the hoop as if he means to take it off the side of the garage, keeping it from his father with the ferocity of a bear protecting its cub. "Good! Good!" shouts Bernard. "That's the spirit!" Suzanne watches from the kitchen window.

After Orlando's father finally leaves for work, his mother asks him to replace the burnt-out bulb in the hall that she can't reach without stilts.

Orlando climbs up on the stepladder, thinking about how electricity can kill you when you least expect it.

"She's all right, you know," says Orlando's mother. "She's in Heaven, and she's safe and happy."

He looks down at her. "What?"

"Sorrel. I know you've been anxious about her, but you don't have to be. She's absolutely fine. And she doesn't want you to worry. Not at all."

It's news to him that he was concerned about Sorrel's afterlife. But, of course, his mother doesn't know that if he were worried about Sorrel it wouldn't be because he was afraid that she isn't flapping her wings and playing a harp somewhere in the clouds, but because he was afraid that she isn't.

"Right," says Orlando. "Thanks, Mom. That's good to know."

"If that's sarcasm, you're not funny," says his mother. "It is good to know."

"So how did you find out that she's happy and everything?" Not that he needs to ask.

Suzanne Gwinnet talks to God. She's always been a churchgoer, but after Raylan died ten years ago, she started talking to Him on a daily basis. God is always reassuring. Raylan, too, is safe and happy and doesn't want anyone to worry about him, but he does like his mother to keep in touch.

"I've been praying for her since— since she passed." As if Sorrel had been walking down the high street and just kept on going. His mother takes the old bulb from him and hands him the new one. "And then this morning I was working in the garden when the most beautiful butterfly landed on my hand. It looked like a painting by one of those Frenchmen. You know what I mean? Colours splotched all over and kind of out of focus? It just sat there. That's when I remembered how I always said Sorrel was like a beautiful butterfly. You remember that? And I realized it was a sign. A sign that she's where she's meant to be. That she's all right." A divine text message. "She wanted you to know."

Only half teasing, he says, "How come she didn't tell me herself?"

"Because miracles aren't wasted on doubters." Suzanne steps back as he climbs down from the ladder. "Because you don't believe she could."

That's not the only thing he doesn't believe. Orlando admires and respects his mother's faith – it's as generous and kind as she is, and has made it possible for her to cope with all the disappointments and heartache that God, in His wisdom, has directed her way – but he is a twenty-first-century boy who doesn't believe in any kind of mumbo-jumbo. Mumbo-jumbo being anything not based on fact and reason. Mumbo-jumbo is superstition and wishful thinking; the beliefs people turn to when reality betrays them; the sort of thing you would have expected to hear by the flickering firelight in a prehistoric cave while the winter winds roared outside and the night hunters howled. And that includes angels and signs from God – and ghosts. A flutter of butterflies the size of a jet plane could land on him and Orlando still wouldn't believe it was Sorrel messaging him through the dimensions of space and time. Sorrel could run beside him every morning and evening, her ponytail bouncing and her voice incessant, and he still wouldn't believe her spirit had come back to haunt him. Indeed, he has put the incident when she did run beside him very firmly out of his mind. It was an aberration. No more than over-exertion on a hot afternoon after a day spent sitting out in the sun. No more than the delayed effects of shock. A symptom of all the daily stress he lives with – most of which is called Dad.

Any time Suzanne Gwinnet starts talking about messages from God or feeling Raylan's presence or saying that she knows her son is well and happy, Bernard Gwinnet stops her with a "Don't talk like a fool, Suzanne. Dead is dead." And storms out of the room. But Orlando wishes he did believe – believed that Raylan, Ruben's dad and Sorrel still exist. That Celeste's mother is right and death isn't the end; that his own mother is right and everything follows God's plan, even if we don't know what that plan is or could possibly be. And he's never wished it as much as he wishes it now.

The afternoon turns into evening; the evening into

night; the night moves on towards morning. The neighbourhood is quiet and dark, everyone asleep or watching TV with the sound down, the lights off and the curtains drawn. His father's out keeping the county safe; his mother's gone to bed. Orlando sits alone in his room, watching a recorded performance of "Revelations" by the Alvin Ailey American Dance Theater.

Normally, he would be transfixed by the dancing, but tonight he keeps thinking about his mother's butterfly.

The house creaks, the wind stirs the leaves, a dog barks somewhere down the road. Orlando stops the show, and yawns. He glances at his computer; it's two a.m. Time to stop thinking about butterflies and get some sleep. And then a movement outside the window catches his attention. It looks as if there's something in the oak tree, but it's hard to tell what because of the light in the room and how tired he suddenly feels and the distance of the tree from the house. The son of a policeman, Orlando has been raised cautious if not actually suspicious. It's probably a cat or something caught in the branches, but just to be on the safe side he puts his laptop on the bedside table and walks over to the window. He puts a hand to the side of his head and his face close to the glass.

And there is Sorrel Groober. Or what, through the window and fatigue and the darkness, looks like Sorrel

Groober. She isn't running now, she's sitting cross-legged in the tree, as casual as someone sitting on a sofa and not at the thin end of a branch several yards in the air. Tonight she is wearing shabby jeans and a boy's flannel shirt (the sort of clothes he always thought she wouldn't be caught dead in) and eating an ice cream (a food she never ate, especially not, he assumes, at two a.m.).

Orlando's first thought is: *Whose shirt is she wearing? Did it belong to that jerk Mike Shoehorn? Or to one of the twins?* His second thought is: *Why would a ghost be eating anything? Ghosts don't have bodies.*

Never mind being haunted; he's starting to spook himself. And so decides to open the window for a closer look, to see what's really there. It may be because of a recent rain, but the window seems to be stuck. He presses the heels of his hands against the frame and pushes with all his considerable strength, straining and looking towards the ceiling. The sash finally gives, but when he sticks out his head there is no one there – nothing caught in the branches, no lurking cat. He ignores the little wave of relief he feels, shuts the window again, closes the blinds and turns back to the room.

Sorrel is sitting at his desk, the laptop now in front of her and back on, and her eyes on the screen.

He knows he shouldn't talk to her, she isn't real, but,

as if some outside force has control of his mind, he hears himself say, "What are you doing here?"

She looks over. "What do you think? I'm doing some of the trillion things I never did before. Never ate ice cream. Never wore scruffy clothes. Never sat in a tree. What about you? What are you doing?" She nods to the computer. "I never knew you were into dance. How come you kept it a secret? This is some pretty cool stuff."

"How the hell did you get in here?"

Sorrel makes an exaggerated *um-duh* face. "You don't think I needed you to open the window for me, do you? I'm kind of non-corporeal these days. The physical laws that govern you don't govern me."

"I wasn't opening the window for you." So now he's not just talking to her, he's snapping at her as well. "I was opening it for me."

"Oh really?" Sorrel smirks. "Going somewhere? Get yourself a jetpack since I saw you last?"

This is totally ludicrous. There's no one else here, and even if there were (which there isn't), Orlando certainly doesn't have to explain himself to her. "You'll have to get out," says Orlando. "It's late. I'm tired. I'm going to bed."

"You should be tired the way you were shooting those baskets with your dad. He's lucky you had a ball in your hand, and not a gun."

"It's a game," says Orlando. "You play to win."

"And it helps with the stress," says Sorrel. "I did yoga to de-stress from living with my mother. So I get it. Your dad's not exactly the Dalai Lama, is he? Meryl the Peril's pretty intense, but your dad could stress out a tree."

Orlando pulls down the bedcovers. "I want to go to sleep. Now."

He might as well have saved his breath.

"But you weren't mellowing out this afternoon. You were angry because he made you play. So here's my question—" she leans towards him— "if basketball isn't a release, what is?"

"You leaving five minutes ago."

She makes a face. *In your dreams.* "It's funny, you know, but I always figured you really liked basketball. I guess 'cause you're the big basketball star. Only you don't, do you?" She gives him a knowing smile. "And it's not the only thing you don't like. Something else you kept quiet about. I mean, everybody knows my mom made me nuts, but you never said anything about your da—"

"That's enough." He snatches the laptop from in front of her, shuts it down and puts it back on the bedside table. "I'm turning out the light. I'm going to bed."

She shrugs. "So be my guest."

Orlando switches off the lamp and gets into bed. He

closes his eyes, but he knows there's no way he'll ever sleep. He's too wound up now; so wound up that he could swear he hears Sorrel breathing in the corner. Is she watching him? Is she going to stay there all night? He reaches over and turns on the bedside light. There's no one at the desk.

Of course there isn't; ghosts don't breathe.

12

New Hope for the Living

~

August

It's the sort of Sunday afternoon that makes people abandon their TVs, computers and home-improvement projects to be outside. Protected from the sun by glasses, creams and hats, they flock to pools and beaches; parks and picnic grounds; backyards and decks. Tennis, boating, white-water-rafting, hang-gliding, golf, mountain climbing, abseiling, even weeding; they'll do anything – as long as they do it under that big blue sky. Music, laughter and the smoke from scores of barbecues fill the air. It seems as if the whole world is out of doors and having a party. Celeste is in her room.

Celeste's room – or her side of it at least (Astra's could only be described as a mirror image if the mirror has been shattered into hundreds of pieces) – is organized and tidy, if idiosyncratic – rather like Celeste herself. There is a shelf of books, a shelf of CDs and a small collection of vinyls (given to her by her father). The clothes in her chest of drawers are all neatly folded; the clothes on her side of the closet neatly hung, the shoes underneath them lined up on a metal rack. Each of her knick-knacks has its own place and is regularly dusted. But there are strings of fairy lights around the window and crisscrossing the ceiling over her bed, and the walls are decorated with the framed sheet music of some of her favourite songs rather than the usual posters and prints. The effect is personal and homey (as opposed to Astra's effect of chaos and destruction). Right now, Celeste is sitting on the floor, playing a song on her guitar. This is how and where she spends most of her free time. Keeping well away from her mother and her sister. She doesn't feel bad for avoiding her sister – Astra is always in a mood, and it's rarely a good one. She does have guilt about avoiding her mother, but the truth is that, though this is something she would never say either silently or out loud, she doesn't always feel like being around Lilah. Her mother has a knack for making Celeste feel that she's bound to do or say the wrong thing – or already has.

The family shopping trip was something of a disappointment for Lilah, if not an outright failure. Celeste, as was noticed, never really got into the spirit of it. Astra was excited and chatty once they got to the mall, but Celeste was quiet and bored. She kept her mother and sister waiting outside the changing room for so long that Astra nearly fainted with hunger and Lilah began to worry that the absence of Sorrel has actually made Celeste more selfish than she'd been, which wasn't what she'd expected. To top it all off, Celeste, who usually listens to her mother's advice, bought not just one item that Lilah had advised her against but four, paying for the extra three herself. "I'm sure you know best," Lilah told her with a smile, making it clear that Celeste didn't.

Lilah, however, is a professional saleswoman; faint heart never clinched an important sale. And so, rather than discourage her, those small acts of rebellion have made Celeste's mother even more determined to break what she considers the unhealthy hold Sorrel Groober had over Celeste – and, apparently, continues to have. Her attempts to separate them when Sorrel was alive didn't succeed, but she has no intention of being defeated by someone who is dead. Time to let go. And so Lilah has encouraged Celeste to get out more. Using a gentle combination of bribery and guilt, she persuaded Celeste to accompany her to one party, two barbecues, a church fair, a brunch and the Skidmore and Pulaski Real Estate Boat Ride – events where she knew there would be other teenagers (though nothing came of any of them). Not nagging, of course, but suggesting (often and a lot), she convinced

Celeste to invite Orlando and Ruben over to watch a film (Ruben couldn't make it and Orlando fell asleep). Today Lilah is using a different technique.

Celeste is singing softly to herself when the door to her bedroom opens and her mother steps in, smiling. Like most of us, Lilah Redwing has a smile for every occasion. This is her selling-a-house-that's-been-on-the-market-for-two-years-and-has-mould-in-the-basement smile. The technique she's using today is deceit. "What are you doing, darling?"

This is another reason why Celeste doesn't always want to be around her mother. What does she think she's doing? Celeste is tempted to say, *Sitting on my bed, playing my guitar.* "Just messing around," says Celeste.

Lilah's smile intensifies. Besides the mould in the basement, there are raccoons in the attic. "Shouldn't you be getting ready, darling?"

"Ready?" echoes Celeste. "I'm sorry, are we going somewhere?"

Her mother laughs. "Don't tell me you've forgotten. Really, you girls…" She shakes her head. *The things mothers have to put up with.* "I know I told you. Iris Moon is coming to lunch."

Celeste frowns. "Iris Moon?" She should have known there was some reason Lilah is home on a Sunday; it's usually her day to see her friends if there aren't any houses to be shown.

"Yes, Iris Moon." Lilah's laugh is like a picture over that damp patch on the wall. "You must remember. She's quite an important figure in the community. I just sold her mother's house over on Old Mill Road?"

Celeste rests the guitar across her lap, trying to coax this memory out of the corner where it seems to be hiding. The name Iris Moon is familiar, possibly because she's such an important figure in the community – but not because Celeste knew she was coming for lunch. "You did?"

"Yes, I did. Remember? 'It's still Summer,' I said. 'It'll be winter soon enough so we should take advantage of this beautiful weather to eat out on the patio more.'" She pauses for a second. "And socialize."

Socialize. That sounds ominous. *Iris Moon, Iris Moon,* thinks Celeste. What is she not remembering about Iris Moon? "I guess I thought you meant you were having lunch with her," lies Celeste. "Not me, too."

"Nonsense. I was very clear. It's an occasion. Astra's invited Winnie. And Iris Moon is bringing her sister who's visiting from DC with her son. And I bought all that lovely food at Barbieri's."

"You did?" Her mother never buys lovely food at

Barbieri's. You could buy a sheep for what they charge for a pound of shrimp salad. Maybe two sheep.

"Yes, I did. I told you, it's an occasion. Iris Moon's sister is in the government. It's not every day we have someone to lunch who knows the President."

"Or even every other day," says a voice unheard by Lilah.

Celeste catches her breath, and moves her eyes to the left. Sorrel is sitting on her desk in lotus pose. She is not dressed to meet someone who knows the President; she's dressed to meet someone who repairs automobiles. With effort, Celeste manages not to smile.

"Besides, darling," says Lilah. Coaxing. "You know it was never meant to be just me and Iris. I am doing this for you."

Celeste focuses on her mother again. "What?"

"For you," Lilah repeats. "I've arranged this all for you. I'm sure I told you."

Sorrel groans. "What do you want to bet this is about the nephew? You're lucky it's not legal to sell daughters, or you'd've been gone long ago."

And that's when Celeste remembers what she has been told about Iris Moon — or at least one of her relatives. Iris Moon's nephew is in college, pre-law, and doing extraordinarily well. He has political ambitions.

"So the nephew's coming to lunch, too," says Celeste. Which explains all the lovely food from Barbieri's – and why Celeste was never told about it.

"Well, of course he's coming, too. They can't very well leave him home by himself, can they?" Lilah's smile becomes serious. "And you can't spend the whole Summer sitting in your room playing your guitar, Celeste. How many times do I have to tell you? You need to get out and meet people." Especially boys with promising futures. "Have a life. There's nothing to stop you now." Meaning Sorrel. "You're not going to be young for ever, you know."

"Oh for God's sake, if she didn't get palpitations every time you say you want to join a band you'd have a life and be meeting people all the time." Sorrel slides gracefully from the desk. "And anyway you are still in your teens. You probably have a few good years left. If you don't get hit by a car."

"Celeste?" says Lilah. "Celeste, are you listening to me? Are you going to put on a dress?"

"Ooh," squeals Sorrel. "Does she want you to wear the bright colours or the stripes?"

Celeste smiles. "You mean one of my new outfits?"

"I was thinking of something a little more conservative," says Lilah. "After all, these are people who dine with senators and lobbyists."

Celeste can feel herself getting ready to give in; she usually does. It's always easier to do what her mother wants than go against her. Especially when you've been ambushed like this and have had no time to prepare your defence.

"Tell her to stuff it," says Sorrel. "She's always trying to fix you up with somebody's nephew or son or grandson. What is she, your pimp? I swear, she's almost as bad as my mother. And anyway, it's Sunday afternoon, Cel. You're going to yoga. Like we always did."

Yoga. Celeste had totally forgotten about yoga. She and Sorrel would spend Saturday night at one or the other's house, mooch around in their pyjamas all Sunday morning, and then go together to the yoga class in the room above the hardware store. Sorrel loved yoga; Celeste likes it okay, but mainly she went because Sorrel did. She hasn't been back since Sorrel died; it never occurred to her to go without her. Celeste is the only member of the class who isn't slim and who is only slightly more flexible than steel. That didn't matter when her black mat was stretched out next to Sorrel's green one. She could do anything, go anywhere when she was with Sorrel; Sorrel was like a free pass to life – accepted everywhere and welcomed with open arms. Sorrel showed her how to make an advantage out of being herself. Sorrel said she wasn't odd, she was different – original, exceptional, unique. Celeste on her own is self-conscious and unsure. And very tall for a girl.

"Celeste? What's wrong with you?" demands her mother, her smile hardening. "Are you going to get dressed? They'll be here soon."

But of course, Celeste isn't on her own any more. Sorrel is keeping an eye on her. Sorrel is giving her a way to get out of this stupid lunch.

"I can't. I'm sorry." Celeste puts her guitar aside and stands up. "It's Sunday, Mom. I have my yoga class. I have to go."

"Surely you can miss one class." If Lilah were ever home on Sundays she would know how true that is. "As a favour. To me. I told everyone you'd be here."

"I'm really sorry, Mom. I have to go. I already paid." Neither of those statements is actually true. "And, besides, it's important to keep up."

Lilah sighs, but it's a sigh of compromise. "Just make sure you're back in time for dessert."

When the door shuts behind her mother, Celeste finally turns to face Sorrel. There's no one there.

But she can hear Sorrel laugh. *Job done*.

13

Lonely No More

The months since he found his mother in the bathtub haven't been easy for Ruben. The eye of a hurricane is the part where the winds are light and the sky is clear – the calm within the storm that rages around it. Sylvia Rossi is like the hurricane's eye. Safe and protected, her life is relatively undisturbed. Which isn't something that can be said for her son's life. Ruben's life has been torn apart and battered by his mother's fears. Now everything he does has to accommodate her. He's even stopped painting. Because it seemed too much like fiddling while Rome was burning to the ground, the only art he's done are nervous doodles when he can't distract himself from worrying about Sylvia – spiky characters with wide, wild eyes and expressions of panic. To fill the empty space, he's thrown himself into a variety of activities besides his job to keep himself busy and have good excuses for not seeing his friends. During school it was clubs and community service; during vacation he gives a few hours a week to walking dogs for the animal shelter and works in the garden so at least the house looks normal on the outside. But no matter how busy he is, Ruben is still as isolated and alone as the sole shipwreck survivor marooned on an uncharted island. And with as little hope of rescue.

This morning he's thinning out the bedding plants, and missing his old self even more than usual. Each plant he removes he puts in a plastic container, and fits into a cardboard box, to be taken to his father's grave. Ruben visits Enzo every week or two; there's no need for both of them to be lonely. It's as he's finishing his work that he has the idea to bring a few plants to Mrs Gwinnet. Orlando once joked that after Raylan was killed his mother discovered Jesus and geraniums; the only time she doesn't work in her garden is when there's snow on the ground. Suzanne Gwinnet wins prizes every year at the local flower show; her garden has even appeared in the Sunday magazine under the heading "Small but Perfectly Formed". The more Ruben thinks about this idea, the more he likes it. He's always been fond of Orlando's mother, and he hasn't seen her since before Sorrel died. It would be a nice gesture. The plants would get a good home. Whistling to himself, he puts the boxes on the passenger seat of the car. He hasn't seen much of Orlando since the funeral, either. Time really flies when you're a paranoid wreck.

Suzanne Gwinnet and Orlando are in the backyard, on their hands and knees in the vegetable patch. The fact that Orlando is weeding with his mother and not shooting baskets or doing push-ups suggests that his father isn't home, but Ruben glances cautiously around, just in case. Officer Gwinnet doesn't approve of much, and boys who aren't into sports are most definitely not an exception to that rule.

Orlando spots Ruben first, coming across the grass with a box of plants in his hands and a smile on his face. "Yo, Rube! What's up?"

"Why, what a nice surprise! It's been ages since I saw you," calls his mother. "Where have you been keeping yourself?"

"Oh, you know," says Ruben. "I've been pretty busy."

"And how's your mom? I never seem to run into her in town any more."

"She's great," Ruben not-quite lies. "She's busy, too. You know, with her writing. She says hello."

Suzanne gets to her feet, brushing her hands on the dungarees she wears when she's gardening. "Well, tell her I say hello back."

They both seem glad to see him; maybe as glad as he is to see them. Back in the real world where people go out in the sun. All systems normal.

Ruben holds out the box. "I was thinning out our beds, and I thought maybe you could use these."

"Why, isn't that thoughtful. Thank you." She puts the box in the shade, brings them iced tea, and vanishes into the house where, it seems, she has things to do.

Ruben and Orlando sit at the picnic table. They're a little awkward at first – *Where do the days go? What you been up to? How are things? Summer's almost over* – but they relax soon enough. Orlando has lifeguard stories to swap for bookshop ones. They sip their tea and laugh, as if nothing has changed between them.

And then, pretty much apropos of nothing, Orlando says, "Remember that time Sorrel said she thought a slam dunk was a doughnut?" He laughs. "Man, did that crack us up or what?"

"I forgot that." Ruben watches the ice bob in his glass. "I forgot how funny she could be."

"Me, too." Orlando nods. "Sometimes, you know..." Orlando, too, seems to be watching what the ice in his glass is doing. "Sometimes it doesn't seem possible she's really dead. Sometimes I kind of forget. And..."

"Yeah," says Ruben. "So do I." Though not for want of trying.

"I'm always thinking I'm going to see her, you know?"

Orlando's eyes now are focused on a point to the right of Ruben's head. "That I'm going to bump into her on the street. Or look out the window and she'll be coming up the sidewalk."

Ruben, still looking at his glass, nods. "I know what you mean."

"There are even times when…" Orlando laughs. "Times when I almost think I do see her."

Ruben looks at him. "You do?" Sunlight glints off their glasses; next door someone turns on a sprinkler and small children shriek. Ruben takes a conscious breath. Now he knows why he's here. To stop feeling so alone. To talk to Orlando. To tell him about seeing Sorrel. To exorcise her once and for all. If he tells Orlando, Orlando will tell him that she's just his imagination and she'll disappear once and for all. Ruben hesitates, trying to get his words together so they don't sound crazy spoken out loud while sitting at a picnic table on a sunny afternoon.

His hesitation lasts too long. Just as he starts to answer – just as he says, "Well…" – Bernard Gwinnet's car pulls into the driveway. Ruben and Orlando both turn to look at it.

And so the moment passes, as moments do. Ruben feels the sun on his head and the cool wetness of the glass in his hand, and hears the car engine turn off and the door open.

"I better go." He stands up. "I have stuff in the car that

I have to get in the ground."

"Right." Orlando stands up, too. "Hey, I'm glad you stopped by. I'll see you soon, yeah?"

"Yeah," says Ruben, "I'll give you a call."

Enzo Rossi is buried in the small cemetery just outside of Peakston. Sylvia comes on the anniversaries of his birth and death, but these more frequent visits are just for Ruben – so Enzo knows how much he is missed.

He leaves the car in the parking area by the entrance and walks to the grave. He doesn't hurry, following the narrow pathways, stopping now and then to read the inscription on a headstone. *Precious daughter... Cherished father... Gone to Heaven... Only sleeping... An empty tale... A morning flower... At rest... At peace... Safe with God... Our loss is Heaven's gain...* Until he finally reaches the one that says *Enzo Rossi, Beloved Husband and Father.*

Ruben puts the box and the trowel down on the ground, then takes an apple he brought from home and sets it on the headstone. His father loved apples. Ruben is thinking about that, about how his father would eat even the apple's core and joke that he'd be sprouting apple trees after they put him in the earth, when someone speaks.

"You know what they're going to put on my headstone? Take a guess."

Ruben stiffens, but looks towards the voice. Sorrel is sitting on the stone marking the final resting place of Johnathan Webster and his wife Sandra – *Together again* – her feet tucked under her and an elaborate bouquet of flowers in her hand. Would she have appeared if he had managed to tell Orlando about these visitations? Now he'll never know.

"You don't want to guess?" says Sorrel. "You're no fun." She touches the bouquet to her head. "Okay, I'll guess. I figure it'll probably be something like, *After all we did for her, this is how she thanks us.*" Sorrel laughs. "Or, maybe, *If we'd known this was going to happen we wouldn't have spent all that money on her teeth.*"

"Is that a joke?"

"Not completely. My mom would think that for sure. She's a total scorekeeper. All the time and effort she put into making me beautiful so I could be famous and I go and die young. But not my dad. He's not petty like that." The flowers sway, thoughtfully. "Well, probably not my dad. But you never know." Sorrel winks, shaking the bouquet. "People are full of surprises, aren't they?"

Even after they're dead.

"They're your parents," says Ruben. "They love you."

"Love can have multiple personalities," says Sorrel. She poses the bouquet coquettishly against her cheek.

"Don't you think?"

Ruben glances around to make certain there's no one who can hear him. There are quite a few visitors on this sunny morning, but none of them are close, and all of them are occupied tending their own loved ones' graves. "Why are you here, Sorrel?"

She spreads her arms. "Where else would I be? It's a cemetery. I'm dead, remember?"

And he's the one who's forgotten that?

"Yeah, I know you're dead. But this isn't your cemetery. You're buried miles away. Shouldn't you be hanging out there?" As if there is a shred of logic in what he's saying, as if that makes the whole thing sensible.

She shrugs. "Maybe I like this one better."

"Why are you following me around? Why don't you leave me alone?"

"You're my friend. I like to talk to you." She swings her feet over the headstone. "And it's a lot easier to do now than when I was alive. When I was alive I was lucky to see you in school. You were always doing something, always so busy. *Can't do this. Can't do that. Have to take a rain check. Maybe next week. I'll let you know.*" She points the bouquet at him. Accusingly. "Or slamming the door in my face."

She makes it sound as if he slammed the door in her face all the time. "I don't want to talk about that." He sees

123

a couple coming towards him, two women maybe ten yards up the path, and bends his head so that, if they're looking, they'll think that he's praying.

"Why not? Why don't you want to talk about it?" She gives him one of her melt-your-heart smiles. "Now you can tell me why you started acting so weird. That's one of the benefits of death. Everybody knows they can trust you with their secrets."

"Yeah, only you can't say you'll take them to the grave," says Ruben. "Not when you won't stay in your grave."

She reaches down and pulls a rose from the bouquet. "Believe me, Ruben, grave or no grave I know how to keep a secret. You think I didn't have secrets? You think everybody doesn't? What makes you think you're so special? You'd be amazed the things you don't know about people you think you know well."

"Go away, Sorrel. Now. Put those flowers down and leave." Suddenly the cemetery seems very busy, people everywhere he looks.

"You really have to lighten up, you know? It's not healthy to be so uptight." She takes the rose she plucked from the bouquet and throws it at him. "And anyway, we've had this conversation before, Ruben. I wouldn't leave then and I won't leave now."

She always was stubborn.

14

Orlando Has More than One Dead Child to Deal with

It almost looks like a commercial. Three people – mother, father, son – sitting on their colonial-style chairs, around their colonial-style table, plates in front of them, forks in hand, knives at the ready. A colonial-style lamp hangs over them, casting a soft light that doesn't reach into the corners of the room. It's obviously not a commercial, however, because no one is smiling or even pretending to be having a good time. Officer Gwinnet is talking, accompanied by the occasional murmured response from his wife.

The Gwinnets are having supper, an activity only slightly less stressful than walking a tightrope between skyscrapers while juggling eggs. Officer Gwinnet works shifts, so he isn't always home in the evenings. When he isn't home, if Orlando and his mother eat together they listen to music and talk about this and that; if they don't eat together, Suzanne will have her meal in front of the TV, watching a programme she likes, and Orlando will have his in his room, watching something he likes. When Officer Gwinnet is home he insists that the three of them eat together, at the kitchen table, the way a family should, having intelligent conversation, and not listening to the crappy music his wife favours or watching some idiot showing off on the TV. Families, like societies, need rules, and Bernard Gwinnet has provided his family with enough to satisfy the fussiest bureaucracy. It goes without saying that he has no idea that, in his absence, the rules he's put in place so assiduously are flouted wilfully and often.

Normally, Orlando listens when his father is speaking (it's dangerous not to; there's always a chance he'll be quizzed on it later), but recently he's found it difficult to concentrate on anything for long. His mind wanders from one thought to another as if searching for just the right one instead of focusing on whatever's at hand. Tonight he's so preoccupied that he only knows his father has been trying to get his attention when something hits the table with such force that the dishes all jump and the bottle of ketchup falls over. There's a sharp intake of breath from his mother. Orlando looks up.

"What's wrong with you, boy? You've had your head up your butt for days. Sulky as a girl." Officer Gwinnet is glaring at Orlando as if he's been caught breaking into an off-license, an offence the elder Gwinnet views as being on a par with being anything like a girl. Obviously, what slammed against the table was his father's fist. "I was talking to you."

"I'm sorry, Dad." Which is certainly true; his father's displeasure is the last thing Orlando or his mother either wants or needs, even if it is one of the things that comes to them far more readily than anything else. The tyranny of Bernard Gwinnet's moods runs their lives. "I was just thinking of something."

"I presume it's something a hell of a lot more interesting than anything I might have to say." Still glaring at his son, Officer Gwinnet stabs the last piece of steak on his plate with his fork as if he's making sure it's dead. "Well, if it's that interesting, I'm sure your mother and I would like to hear what it is. Wouldn't we, Suzanne?" He waves the pink chunk of flesh at Orlando. "Come on. Enlighten us."

Orlando's pretty sure they wouldn't want to hear what he was thinking. It would worry his mother, who has enough to worry about; and it would infuriate his father, who has more than enough to be furious about. What he was thinking of right then was Sorrel. For a change.

"We're waiting," says his father. "What was so engrossing?"

"It was nothing, Dad. Just stuff."

Today, at the lake, he thought he saw Sorrel again. She was sitting on a multi-coloured beach towel decorated with chameleons. Sorrel was known for being a meticulous and coordinated dresser like her mother, but today she was wearing a fraying, floppy straw hat, plaid boy's swim trunks and a white halter top. He couldn't see the title of the book she was reading, but he did see that her nails were silver. She looked unbelievably fantastic. And so relaxed, as if she didn't have a care in the world – which was not a look she'd monopolized in her lifetime. He was overwhelmed with the desire to touch her, to speak to her. When he's seen her before he's wanted to run away from her; this time he wanted to run to her. He jumped down from his station and nearly landed on a woman who wanted to know the lake policy on inflatables. When he finally got away from her, Sorrel had picked up her things and was almost at the pavilion. Orlando ran. He could sense people turning to watch him, thinking there was some emergency – somebody drowning on the deck – but he didn't care. He galloped across the beach and sped past the café. Orlando is an accomplished runner, but somehow she always stayed several yards ahead of him. As his feet hit the tarmac of the car park he shouted, "Sorrel! Sorrel! Wait up!" Which was when he realized there was no one there.

His father, however, has not disappeared, but is still glowering at him. "Stuff? What stuff?"

"Just stuff," he says now. "There's going to be a lot to do this year."

"You bet your sorry ass there is. This is a big year for you." Bernard's cutlery clanks after every sentence. "You better be on the ball, mister. This isn't the time for you to get moody and have *stuff* on your mind. You have to be sharp and focused." There's a pool of bloody juice where his meat used to be. He pushes away his plate. "You haven't been skipping your extra practice, have you?"

Suzanne lifts the salad bowl and wants to know if anyone wants more.

"I've never missed a session," says Orlando.

"I hope not. And you better not be sloppy about your training. You can't drop the ball now." Not unless it's straight through the hoop. "You just better be keeping up. You know I can always check."

Oh, he knows that. Officer Gwinnet is acquainted or on a first-name basis with everybody from the mayor to the town clerk, from the superintendent of schools to the janitor – and everyone in between. And the few people he doesn't know know him. He's on the same bowling team as the basketball coach, the football coach and the guidance counsellor. Orlando might as well be living with the head of the FBI; there's nothing he does in this town, or even in the county, that his father can't (and usually won't) find out about. When he was younger, if Orlando gave some grown-up lip, accidentally broke something, took a shortcut through someone else's property – anything, no matter how big or how small – his father would know about it before Orlando got home. It's always been like that, but since Raylan was killed it's been much worse. Officer Gwinnet watches Orlando like a hawk watching a rabbit. Even last year when Orlando broke the diet his father set for him and got a burger, the manager of the McDonald's called Officer Gwinnet to tell him while Orlando was still in the restaurant. And when the other guys will sneak a beer or smoke a spliff while they're watching a movie, Orlando sticks with plain old water and air in case it turns out that walls can talk and also use the phone. When Orlando and his mother do go against Officer Gwinnet, they cover their tracks carefully and make very sure there are no witnesses. Which is something they've become very good at over the years. A small but solid example of the law promoting crime.

"No worries, Dad. I'm keeping up with everything."

"You better be. We can't afford for you to slack off now. You have your provisional, but you're not in yet."

"I'm not slacking off, Dad. I just have a lot to think about."

Officer Gwinnet taps his fingers on the table, waiting for dessert. "There's only one thing should be on your mind, and that's UCLA." The college of Bernard Gwinnet's choice. But being picked for the team on condition that he continues to perform is not the same as being on the team. "This next year is the rehearsal. If you mess up now, it's over."

Orlando's mother gets up and starts clearing the dishes. Orlando would help her if his father weren't here, but Officer Gwinnet is here – and he believes that each member of the family has a job. His job is to maintain law and order in the county and support and manage his family; his wife's is to take care of that family and the house in which they live. Orlando's "job" (it has been pointed out more than once) is to become a professional basketball player, not do the dishes. Neither Suzanne's nor Orlando's job description includes "giving Bernard a hard time".

In the momentary silence, Suzanne says, "Guess who I ran into today." She says this brightly, changing the subject.

"Don't keep us in suspense, Suzanne." Her husband sounds so bored you'd think she'd been doing all the talking for the last forty minutes. "Tell us."

"Meryl Groober." She sets the dishes on the counter. "Poor thing. She still doesn't look like herself. I don't think she's slept much since the tragedy."

Orlando's heart groans. Of course. Who else could it possibly be? If they lived in a city of millions and not a town of thousands Meryl Groober is still the one person his mother would run into. Even before his father responds, Orlando knows that, as diversionary tactics go, this one is like waving a slab of raw meat at a charging lion, hoping to make it go away. Dead children are a sensitive issue for his father.

"Nothing poor about her," snaps Officer Gwinnet. "And it's not a tragedy, it's a self-inflicted wound. She brought it on herself."

Orlando wills his mother not to answer, to change the subject again to something less charged – like national health insurance or abortion (two topics about which her husband feels especially strongly). But, of course, if she could read minds she probably would never have married his father.

"Oh, Bernard, I don't think that's true. I know what you think, but I still believe it was an accident."

"You can believe what you want," says her husband, "but I told you, that's not what we on the force believe."

Orlando is now giving them his complete attention. He has no idea what they're talking about, though he has the uneasy feeling he could make a good guess. "What? What wasn't an accident?"

"Don't pay him any mind," his mother says to Orlando. To her husband she says, "What does it matter, Bernard? Whatever did happen that night, it was still a terrible thing. It's still a tragedy." She puts a slice of pie in front of him, and a bowl of fruit salad in front of Orlando. "Losing their daughter like that is tearing those poor people apart."

"I know what it's like to lose a child, Suzanne. There's not a day goes by that I don't live through that hell." As if he lives through that hell alone; as if his wife and son feel nothing and never have. "But there's a big difference between an accident and a suicide. Raylan was unlucky." He picks up his fork, holding it in front of him like a gun. "Sorrel Groober didn't just happen to be in the wrong place at the wrong time." Which would be passed out drunk without a seat belt in the passenger seat of a car driven by a girl who'd been drinking nearly as much as you. No one has ever said out loud that it was Officer Gwinnet who dropped the ball that time, not realizing that Raylan liked to drink and break curfew and drive fast with his girlfriend. And no one has ever corrected his opinion that it was all the girlfriend's fault. "A suicide, it's the parents who are to blame. One way or another, they drove her to it."

Orlando has a sudden image of Sorrel sitting in the back seat of the Groobers' hatchback, being driven to the open arms of Death.

"If it was a suicide," murmurs his mother. "You don't know for sure."

Orlando shakes off the image of Sorrel speeding towards Death and turns to his father. "Are you saying you think Sorrel killed herself? Why are you saying that?"

"Because it's probably true." Officer Gwinnet stabs at his pie. "Rain or no rain, there was no way she didn't see what was coming. She just waited till the last second and jumped out in front of the car. Lucky she didn't kill the driver."

"He's full of it." Standing behind his father, wearing an ivory tutu, ivory leotard and ivory pointe shoes, and not being driven anywhere, is Sorrel. She's in first position. "Trust me. I was there. I know what happened."

Orlando manages not to let his jaw drop, but his spoon clatters to the floor.

"For God's sake, boy! Can't you even hold a simple utensil any more?"

"Sorry." If he could glue his eyes to the tabletop, he would.

"No harm done," says his mother. "I'll bring you another one."

"Bad parenting always shows," his father goes on. "People like them. Weak. Over-indulgent. Him the college professor and her all la-di-da. Making that girl think she was something special and could do what she wanted just because she had a pretty face."

Sorrel moves seamlessly to second then to third position. "That's not true, either. But even if it was, it's better than thinking you know everything because you wear a badge."

Oblivious, his father goes on. "Think they're better than everybody else, the Groobers. And that girl, she looked like one of them dolls."

"Crapola." Sorrel does a *grand plié*. "I looked much better than any doll."

"Probably spoiled the girl till she was as rotten as apples left on the ground all winter," says Officer Gwinnet, unaware that he's been contradicted. "But they'd never see that, would they? Too up their own butts. Good parents know their kids. They know what's going on with them."

Suzanne returns to the table with her own slice of pie and a spoon for Orlando.

Orlando is mentally singing something very loudly – one of the old rock anthems that he likes to play while he's running – trying to drown out his father's words (or at least obscure them a bit). But he has to look up to take the spoon from his mother, and sees that now Sorrel is doing *fouetté* turns.

"What the hell are you gawping at?" Pie filling falls from Officer Gwinnet's fork as he shakes it in Orlando's direction. "You look like you've seen a ghost.".

Orlando can't even manage a choked "Of course not". He feels as if his blood has turned to granite. Behind his father, Sorrel moves into a *brisé en arrière*.

"I think Meryl would be grateful if she could see Sorrel's ghost," his mother says as she sits down. Suzanne may not be very aggressive, but she is remarkably intrepid. "At least that would give her a little comfort."

Or maybe not, thinks Orlando as Sorrel executes a *grand jeté* from one end of the kitchen to the other.

"She should've raised her right in the first place," judges Officer Gwinnet. "That's what she should've done. Raise them right and you don't have any problems."

Unless they ignore your strictures about not abusing alcohol, staying out late, dating girls you don't approve of and breaking the speed limit, and then die in a car crash.

Suzanne cuts a dainty triangle from her pastry. "But if you saw how upset she is, Bernard—"

"She'd've ended up a lot more upset if that girl had lived." Officer Gwinnet shovels a large forkful of pie into his mouth. "Believe me. She was trouble, that one. You could tell just by looking at her. I always knew it."

Orlando's eyes are focused on the tablecloth. It's patterned with sailboats, starfish, seagulls, sandcastles and pails and shovels – his mother likes to keep things seasonal. He's particularly intrigued by the sailboats, if only because he wishes one would pull up outside and whisk him away. He is aware of Sorrel doing *brisés volés* in the space between the table on one side of the room and the sink on the other – but he is refusing to look her way. And then, despite his best efforts, he hears his father say (so clearly he might be shouting in his ear): "She was trouble, that one. You could tell just by looking at her."

Sorrel stops dancing. "What the hell does he mean by that?" Orlando's still looking at the tablecloth, but he knows that she's talking to him. "What does he mean? Trouble how? Tell what?"

Does she expect him to answer her? Even if Orlando knew, he wouldn't be able to answer. He's so shocked about what's happening that he's temporarily lost his own power of speech. Has his father forgotten that Orlando went out with Sorrel, that they never stopped being friends?

"Bernard," Suzanne almost whispers. "Orlando—" She remembers Orlando and Sorrel dated even if her husband doesn't. "The poor girl's dead."

"If you ask me, the boy's better off without her," says her husband. "She was a distraction he doesn't need."

"Bernard. Please."

"Don't 'Bernard' me. Being dead doesn't make her an angel."

"And bossing everyone around doesn't mean you're always right," says Sorrel.

Which finally makes Orlando look up. Sorrel is standing a foot or two from Officer Gwinnet, watching him the way you might watch a buzzard pick at the carcass of a puppy. Officer Gwinnet is a man who commands respect from one and all (and demands it). Sorrel was always polite to him and polite about him, never saying what she really thought. Which Orlando now realizes wasn't very much. But that, of course, was when she was alive. She makes a hand gesture that Orlando is pretty sure she never made in her life, and sticks out her tongue.

Oblivious to this, Orlando's mother suddenly jumps up. "You know what," she says, "I think I'll have a cup of tea."

When Orlando looks back to Sorrel, she's disappeared.

And who could blame her?

15

A Day of Firsts

~

September

It's the first day of the new school year.

Celeste stares at the mirror, telling herself that she looks good; that she's okay. "Everything's going to be fine," she tells her reflection. "You're a senior. There's nothing to be nervous about."

Which should be true. She is a senior; she's done this before. Indeed, if we're counting, this is the thirteenth first day of school for Celeste. By now it should be as easy as turning on her phone. And, normally, it would be. Before she met Sorrel, Celeste always found the first day of the school year stressful. New classmates, new teachers; not certain what to expect. Celeste was unsure of herself and considered odd by others. Once she and Sorrel were friends, however, that changed. Sorrel had enough confidence for both of them.

"You're winding yourself up about nothing," she tells her image in the mirror. "It's going to be just like always."

No it won't. If all Celeste had to worry about is new classmates and new teachers, she'd be fine. Today, however, she has the absence of Sorrel to worry about. Everywhere she looks there will be things to remind her. Every corner she turns she'll expect to see Sorrel coming towards her with her model-on-a-runway walk, or expect to hear Sorrel hurrying behind her shouting, "Oi! Wait up!" The school is a minefield of memories: the spot where everything fell out of Sorrel's purse; the place where they always waited for each other; the corner in the library where they were sitting when they got the giggles and were told to leave. Sorrel's locker; Sorrel's favourite table in the cafeteria; Sorrel's favourite spot when they sat outside; the people she liked; the boys she dated; the girls who didn't like her; the teacher who gave her detention.

And, in the midst of it all, Celeste. Celeste alone. Alone and vulnerable. The students and teachers who used to make her feel nervous and insecure will make her feel nervous and insecure again. Without Sorrel, she'll go back to being the odd one out; the one who doesn't fit in.

When she gets to school, she's surprised to find Orlando and Ruben waiting for her.

"We figured today's going to be pretty weird," says Ruben, "so we should kind of band together."

"We didn't want you to think we don't know it could be a little rough for you," says Orlando.

And Celeste doesn't want them to see how grateful she is. "I didn't know you cared," she jokes.

"Of course we do," says Ruben.

Orlando winks. "We just don't always show it."

But once the first bell rings the boys go off in different directions, and Celeste really is on her own. *Be normal*, she tells herself. *It's just another day.* And, to her surprise and relief, everyone else is normal, too. Teachers smile and ask her how she is. *Ready for your last year?* Kids she's friendly with are glad to see her. *Hi. How was your Summer? What classes do you have? Who's your homeroom teacher? You in the orchestra this year?* Almost everyone avoids the topic of dead best friends the way you would avoid a deep hole in the middle of the pavement. The only ones who mention Sorrel are those she hasn't seen since before the accident because they were already away. *Heard what happened. Really sorry. It really sucks.* Celeste goes to her classes and no one whispers when she walks in. She strolls down the hall by herself, trying to appear relaxed, nodding to people she knows, and no one looks the other way. The routine of school takes over, and the morning goes quickly enough. There are periods of as long as five or even ten minutes when Celeste forgets that Sorrel is gone.

At lunch, Celeste sits with girls she knows from the orchestra – the cellist, a viola player and two violinists. In the small world of the Beaconspoint High School orchestra, the Christmas concert will be the major event of the year, which at least gives them all something to talk about that isn't the most recent funeral they attended.

Orlando and Ruben are meeting Celeste after last period to walk home together. Celeste stops in the girls' toilets on her way out, and takes a stall at the end. She's been concentrating so hard on getting through the day and being as normal as sunshine that her mind starts to meander as soon as she sits down. She's thinking about the sign she saw on the bulletin board outside the office – *guitarist/mandolin player wanted for new band* – and wondering if she should try for it and what her mother would say if she did and was actually asked to join when her phone bings: Orlando wanting to know where she is. Celeste texts back that she's on her way, and gets ready to leave. She is aware, vaguely, that a group of girls has come in, talking together noisily, but then, just as she moves her hand to unbolt the door, Celeste hears Sorrel's name.

A voice she can't quite place is telling a story she heard from the Groobers' neighbour – or maybe it was a friend of the Groobers' neighbour – about the night Sorrel died. The neighbour had just come home and was getting out of her car when Sorrel stormed out of the house, shouting that she was eighteen and could do what she wanted. Meryl Groober tried to grab her but she ran off into the rain. The neighbour said Sorrel and her mother were always fighting.

The other girls laugh.

"Well, that makes a historic first, someone fighting with her mother," says one of them. "What's that meant to prove?"

"It doesn't *prove* anything," says the first girl. "But it does make you think, doesn't it? About the other stuff I heard? What if she did step in front of that car on purpose? You know… kill herself…"

Now Celeste recognizes the voice. It belongs to one of the girls who from the first day of kindergarten always made her feel nervous and insecure. Cati Grear, prom-queen-in-waiting, who, until very recently, was the second-prettiest girl at Beaconspoint High. Every cell of her body alert, Celeste stares straight ahead, although all she can see, of course, is the beige metal door in front of her and the graffiti that time and the janitorial staff haven't managed to erase.

Another voice points out that no one really knows what happened, even the driver didn't seem to know, but that everything she read and heard made it sound like an accident.

"I'm just telling you what people are saying," says Cati. "I mean, I know the paper and everything said it was an accident, but, really, where's the proof?"

Someone says she thought the coroner's verdict was the proof.

"Maybe," says Cati. "But coroners can be wrong. My dad says that if the coroner wasn't sure one way or the other she'd probably go for accident to spare the family."

"Spare them what?" asks another girl. "Sorrel's still dead."

"Or it could mean they do know for sure," says someone else. "That's why they decided it was an accident."

"I'm just saying what I heard," Cati repeats. "And the woman who was driving the car? She said Sorrel just walked right out in front of her. I mean, okay, it was night and it was raining, but it wasn't a monsoon. You could see the lights."

Gathered at the sinks like animals at a watering hole, the girls continue to talk. Some continue to disagree with Cati. Haven't they all walked into things because they were looking at their phones and not paying attention? It's practically the millennial disease. One of them walked right into a glass door. Another sprained her ankle because she was reading a text and didn't realize she was stepping off the kerb.

"But none of us walked into traffic," says Cati.

Celeste knows that what Cati's saying isn't true. Not in a million years. She and Sorrel had plans. A future. People who know they have a future don't kill themselves. Her phone bings again. This time it's Ruben. *Where are you?* She ignores it.

There is only one person, of course, who knows exactly what happened that fateful, rainy night. Knows that Sorrel's mother was pushing her to go to the party without Celeste. It had been a while since she broke up with Orlando – when was she going to start dating again? How can a girl with her looks not have a boyfriend? Did she want people to think there was something wrong with her? And that's when Sorrel told her. She didn't want a boyfriend; she wanted a girlfriend. She wanted Celeste. Meryl Groober went into earthquake mode. *I'm going to Celeste's, and you can't stop me!* Sorrel screamed back.

Cati holds her ground, but the others all think looking at her phone makes more sense than suicide. Why would Sorrel Groober kill herself? Since she wasn't some poor loser.

"Maybe there was something wrong with her," says Cati. "You know. Mentally."

"I'll tell you who has something wrong with her mentally," says the only person who knows exactly what happened. "That cow does. If it isn't bad news, Cati Grear won't repeat it. She's a viper in the bosom of life."

Celeste, until this moment fairly paralysed with horror, raises her eyes. Sorrel is sitting on top of the stall door, gazing over at the girls at the sinks. She's wearing rolled- up jeans, flip-flops and an old football jersey with tabasco sauce stains on it. And this the girl who was considered not only "best looking" but "most sophisticated" as well. "It hasn't taken her long to recover from the awful shock of my death. I mean, my God, I'm barely in my grave and look at how she's trashing me. I knew when she turned up at my funeral, it was all an act."

"I didn't," whispers Celeste. "I really thought she'd had a change of heart."

"She doesn't have a heart," says Sorrel. "And sometimes I think you have too much. Always wanting to believe the best. Even if there isn't any best. Lots of people are just out for themselves."

Celeste's phone bings a third time.

Sorrel peers down at her. "Aren't you supposed to be meeting the boys?"

"Well, yeah, but I can't leave yet."

"How come?"

She nods towards the door. "I have to wait till they go."

At the sinks, the topic of conversation has moved on to

the homecoming dance. It could be a while before it's over.

"How come?"

This is where feeling nervous and insecure kicks in. Why Sorrel should have watched where she was going and not walked into the road, leaving Celeste all alone. "You know…"

"What? You don't want Cati to know you overheard her? Why not? She's the one who should be ashamed of herself."

This time Celeste's phone rings. Ruben calling.

"Uh-oh," says Sorrel. "You've been rumbled. They're looking at your feet. What are you going to do?"

Celeste could, of course, spend the rest of the afternoon where she is. She could stay here long after Cati and her friends finally leave – just in case they're lingering outside. Waiting to confront her. To accuse her of eavesdropping, of spying on them. Sorrel was always braver than she is. But now, of course, there's only one of them left to be brave.

Celeste taps Answer, and opens the door.

There are five girls standing with their backs to the mirrors. They're not looking at Celeste's feet now, they're looking at her.

"I'm sorry. I got held up. I'm on my way," says Celeste into the phone, and hangs up. She steps past the girls to wash her hands, and they all turn to watch her. "You know what?" she says, looking at Cati Grear in the glass. "I never did like you, but it wasn't until now that I understood why. You're a viper in the bosom of life."

As she marches out the door, she glances over her shoulder.

Sorrel is gone, of course.

She always encouraged Celeste to make her own decisions.

16

There Is Never Any Danger
of Running Out of Things
to Worry About

Only one of Ruben's friends has ever tried to breach Fortress Rossi, and that, of course, was Sorrel. (Sorrel never liked to take no for an answer.) That was long ago last April. Ruben ran into her in town. She'd just come from having her hair trimmed; he'd just come from buying a bulk order of candles at the hardware store. He usually saw her with other people and wasn't used to being alone with her, though not because he didn't want to be. Being alone with Sorrel was something of a dream come true for Ruben (or several dozen dreams), but it made him nervous, too. He was never sure what to say, always wondering if she knew what he secretly wanted to say while praying that he'd keep his mouth shut. They chatted for several minutes on the street, and then she offered him a lift home. If she'd had the entire football team and their pets with her, he would have said yes. They had a nice drive, talking and laughing just as if they weren't alone. They pulled up in front of his house and he thanked her for the ride and she said not to mention it. He opened his door.

But instead of letting him out and driving on, Sorrel cut the engine and announced that she had to use the bathroom, if it was okay with him. She was out of the car before he was.

It wasn't okay with him. The bag of candles was awkward and heavy, so that by the time he did get out of the car she was ahead of him and already gliding towards the house.

"Sorrel, come back." He loped after her, trying not to look as if he was running. Even better than being alone with Sorrel should have been being alone in his house with her. But rather than a dream come true it was now a nightmare. There was no way he could let her inside. Unless he blindfolded her and guided her to the bathroom, she was going to notice how dark it was; how silent; how you couldn't see out of most of the windows. Even if he got her through the house and to the bathroom without realizing how weird everything was, once in there she was going to wonder why the light didn't work. If she didn't notice any of those things – as though she was in a Gaia Pendragon novel and a spell had been cast over her – then there was the problem of Gaia Pendragon herself. Sorrel's parents are front-of-house presentable. Whereas his mother is more like the madwoman in the attic. To complicate his situation even further, it wasn't Sylvia Rossi's idea that his friends never came around any more. She always asked about them. *How's Celeste? Sorrel busy with her modelling? Why doesn't Orlando ever stop by?* If she'd heard Sorrel's voice – and when did you not hear Sorrel's voice? – she might actually have left her room to see her. Probably wearing a foil helmet and a space blanket, just to be on the safe side. The madwoman who'd shuffled out of the attic and was standing at the top of the stairs, shouting hello. "I'm really sorry," he said, "but I'm afraid you can't use the bathroom."

Sorrel stopped short and swung around. "Why not? Don't tell me you keep your pet lion in there."

Fortunately (or unfortunately, depending on how you looked at it), covering for his mother had made him a quick and devious thinker. An artful dodger. "No." Hahaha. "It's broken. Leaks all over."

She started walking again. "So, okay, I'll use the WC by the kitchen."

"You won't believe this," he said, trotting behind her, "but that's not working either."

This time she turned so quickly that he nearly fell into her. He was right, she didn't believe him. "What are you and your mom doing, shitting in the woods with the bears? Peeing in pots?"

"We're waiting for the plumber. He should be here this afternoon."

By then they were almost at the porch. Babbling about how busy the plumber was and how you don't realize how much you take things like toilets for granted until they stop working, he managed to get between her and the house. "Thanks again for the ride," he said. "I'm sorry about the bathroom."

She didn't move. She said, "While I'm here I'd like to say hello to your mom. It's been ages since I saw her."

This was when he knew that she had planned it. Maybe Sorrel hadn't actually gone to town hoping to trap him, but she'd been planning ways to get into the house – waiting for her moment like a professional burglar. She had the sort of looks that often made people think that was all there was to her, but it was like thinking there was nothing more to a cake than the icing, especially one with a file hidden inside for sawing through metal bars. He took a step forward. "She'll be having a nap now." He took another step. "She always needs a break in the afternoon."

Sorrel took a step. Only it wasn't backwards, it was forwards. "You don't know that. She might be up by now."

A million-dollar smile and the determination of an invading army.

"She won't be," he assured her. Another step. "She gets really tired."

"Why can't we just see if she is up?" And again she came towards him.

"Sorrel, please." He was going to just gently turn her around, but either she wouldn't move or he moved too much and instead of propelling her to the kerb he dropped the bag and three cases of household candles fell to the ground. They both stared down at them.

"Candles?" Sorrel looked at him, still puzzled. Or, possibly, just suspicious. "Is there something wrong with your electrics, too?"

"Atmosphere." He bent down and scooped them back into the bag. "You know. For the books. My mother likes to really get in the mood."

Ruben is remembering that afternoon as he prepares for the day, because now he always thinks of Sorrel when he has to leave the house. In case he runs into her. He hasn't in the last few weeks, but that doesn't mean he won't. He knows enough about life by now to know how it works: as trustworthy as a conman.

He is getting ready in the kitchen, of course; the only room except for his where it isn't always midnight during a power cut. In the rest of the house, all the curtains are perpetually drawn, all the blinds perpetually closed, all the doors perpetually shut, but there are no blinds or curtains in the kitchen; his mother never comes in here. Too many electrical appliances. From a woman whose spaghetti sauce was legendary she's become a woman who can't boil water.

He checks himself out in the mirror he's hung over the sink. Head, hair, shirt, smile. He looks okay; clean, neat, presentable – and sane. Today he looks even better than usual. Today, wearing a dark blue jacket and slacks with a crease in them, he looks as distinguished as a teenage boy can. He has a meeting before school with the guidance counsellor to plan his future, and he wants to impress her. He wants to impress himself, too – some days he isn't sure he has a future.

"You're not crazy," he assures his reflection. He definitely doesn't look crazy. "Everything's chill."

Telling himself that he isn't crazy is a ritual Ruben has performed every morning since he found his mother in the bathtub wearing her foil hat, but he's never been more serious about it than he's been since he started seeing Sorrel. Just saying "You're not crazy" always makes him feel better for a while. He's hoping that if he says it enough it will have to be true.

Ruben finishes the mug of coffee on the counter, picks up his new satchel and leaves the brightness of the kitchen for the darkness of the rest of the ground floor. When he reaches the front door he calls, "Bye, Mom," up the stairs, but not too loudly; chances are she'll be asleep by now, exhausted from working till dawn. My mother, the creature of the night.

He steps onto the porch and gazes out on Garibaldi Drive. It's a typical early Autumn day, the kind on which his dad used to take him and Orlando camping. The sun shines, the clouds float overhead, leaves rustle in the breeze. This is where he stops feeling better, and starts feeling wary. He scans the opposite side of the street, then looks to the left and the right. A woman wearing a bathrobe and bedroom slippers is walking her dog, a group of boys are jostling each other along the pavement and the man next door is lying on his stomach in his driveway, trying to coax a cat out from under his car. Coast clear; no ghosts. Ruben starts down the steps.

It could be that he's being overly cautious. It's not like she pops up all the time. She spaces her visits. Not widely enough – fifty or sixty years between would work better for him – but she does space them. Maybe she doesn't want to wear out her welcome. As it is, the time between visitations is just enough for him to think they're over and let his guard down. Which means that he isn't being overly cautious, he's being sensible. Maybe she'll stay away if he's expecting her. Of course, if nothing will keep her away it doesn't matter how cautious he is. How can he avoid her if she knows where he'll be and what he'll be doing? Not that he believes in ghosts; he doesn't. His own guess is that what's happening is a chemical reaction between his worry over his mother, his grief over his dad and his shock over Sorrel. Besides, Sorrel was a serial dater who went out with a lot of boys, but one of those boys was Orlando. Something that never bothered Ruben – for a change she was showing good taste. But it should mean that if she were going to haunt anyone, it should be him and not Ruben. Unless it's Sod's Law: Orlando gets her passionate kisses, and Ruben gets her unquiet spirit.

Once on the pavement, he walks quickly, keeping his eyes on the straight ahead. When he reaches the school grounds he'll be safe. Sorrel was never the biggest fan the education system ever had. She was smart, but she wasn't interested. School is the last place she'd revisit.

Mrs Witten is waiting for him with a cup of coffee from the staffroom, milk and sugar – she hopes that's all right. It's the first time he's sat down with her since his freshman year, but she seems to remember him well.

Knows his grades, knows his test scores, knows his extracurricular activities, know that his mother's a writer, knows he designed the sets for the drama club's production of *Arsenic and Old Lace* last year and *A Midsummer Night's Dream* the year before. Thinks he should get at least a partial scholarship to the college of his choice.

She has his school record and a stack of catalogues on her desk, the best fine arts colleges in the country. So she doesn't know everything about him.

"You're not interested in art any more?" She makes it sound as if he's given up food. "I thought you were so serious about it. Everyone says how much talent you have."

"I know." He does. "I've been back and forth over it for months. That's why I'm only seeing you now. But this Summer I finally decided." Ruben's smile exudes a maturity and confidence he can only hope she believes he possesses. "Once and for all."

"I had the impression art has been your focus since you were very young." Mrs Witten taps her pen against the desk. "What made you change your mind now?"

It's not his mind that's changed. Ruben used to be a free spirit. He does well enough in school, but he wasn't interested in following an academic path to a college major that would lead him to a profession with a high salary, good benefits and a secure future. He'd known he wanted to be a painter from the age of three, when he got his first set of watercolours. A free spirit and a romantic, he read the lives of artists he admired, and filled his head with stories of past art worlds in France, England, Italy and Spain. He was especially drawn to bohemian Paris in the 1920s. He imagined himself living in a garret, selling his paintings along the riverbank, falling asleep listening to the rain beat against the skylights. And even if the world had changed a lot since then, it still had room for artists. He had the talent; he had the drive. Ruben might not get to 1920s Paris, but he could move to twenty-first-century New York or San Francisco, find some job to pay the rent and let him paint. He could even do some street art, murals on buildings, signs of the times.

"I guess I just grew up," says Ruben. Which is one way of putting it, but not, perhaps, the most detailed or the most accurate. "That kind of life's too insecure. For every successful artist you've heard of there are another thirty thousand with an attic full of pictures no one wants. I need a real profession. Something that'll give me a good living and a secure future. Not a career where I might not make any money until I'm dead. And then that's only if I'm lucky."

"So what do you have in mind?" asks Mrs Witten.

"I was thinking maybe business or law," says Ruben.

"Or maybe business law." There is a lot of money to be made representing corporations – they're the barns full of geese laying giant golden eggs. "I've joined the Young Entrepreneurs' Club and I'm on the debate team to hone my powers of persuasion, and this term I'm doing my community service at the law centre in Peakston." And he smiles again, so neither of them can tell how much he dislikes it.

"In that case," says Mrs Witten, "you may still want to consider Harvard."

Ruben says, "Undergraduate, I may stick closer to home."

The first bell rings as he leaves the counsellor's office. The meeting went well. Saying his new direction out loud for the first time makes it right; makes it real. Ruben lopes to his locker, and opens the door. Sorrel Groober is sitting in the space where his coat is meant to go, reading a book on Renaissance art. Which is as much a surprise as the fact that she can fit in his locker. His heart wallops so hard that, if he were able to think, he'd think he was having a stroke.

"You know what I suddenly realized?" She lowers the book and looks over at him. "I actually like knowing stuff. It makes the world so much bigger. And, I don't know, fascinating and alive. I mean, like this?" She holds up the book. "This is thousands of times more interesting than your average photo shoot. Honestly? Your average photo shoot makes peeling mushrooms seem exciting. People don't get it, but a model's just a prop, really. Like the palm tree or the snake or the fake sphinx. Only she's the prop that everybody yells at."

Ruben glances over his shoulder. There are a couple of kids at the end of the corridor, talking together as they walk towards him. "Shhh!" he hisses. "Someone's coming!"

She doesn't shhh. Surprise, surprise. "It's all Meryl the Peril's fault. As per usual," says Sorrel. "She said I shouldn't waste my time on books and school and all that crap. I was going to be this famous model and nobody was going to give two false nails what I thought about anything except make-up and clothes. She said it's better to be beautiful than bright. 'Look at your father,' she'd say. 'Where did being smart ever get him? Teaching at a second-rate community college in the sticks.' Eat your heart out, Albert Einstein, right?"

Ruben can hear himself breathe. Is that a question she expects him to answer?

"I'm trying to make a point here," says Sorrel. "I don't know why you want to do business or law. You've never been interested in those things. You've always known exactly what you wanted to do. I can see now that that's a gift. To be so sure. To have something you really care about. And to actually be able to do it. To have nobody telling you that you have to do something else. How can you dump that gift in the garbage like you're doing?" Apparently she doesn't expect an answer from him, because this time she doesn't give him a chance to make one. "Me, I never wanted to be a model. That's what Meryl wanted to be – only that didn't work out for her. So she took all her ambition and dumped it on me. Which is kind of what you're doing. Only you're taking all your ambition and putting it into something you don't care about. Why are you doing that, Ruben? What's got into you? Do you think you're going to get a second chance to get your life right?"

He can hear voices that don't belong to Sorrel getting closer, but he's afraid to look. Instead, he slams shut the door, and leans his head against it. Stupid. Super stupid. There was no one there. She wasn't all squashed up; she wouldn't fit in there if she wasn't all squashed up. He must have left something hanging. A sweater. A bag. Something. As two girls pass him, Ruben straightens up and slowly opens the door again.

He can smell lilacs (not a scent common to his locker), but there is, of course, no one there.

17

Orlando Has to Hope that It's Easier for the Dead to Keep a Secret than It Is for the Living

Orlando has a secret life. It may not be as interesting or romantic as the secret life of Clark Kent – mild-mannered reporter in his day job, Superman fighting for truth, justice and the American way whenever needed, which is fairly often – but it requires just as much subterfuge and deceit to keep anyone from finding out about it. Possibly more. Orlando assumes that among Superman's special powers are nerves of steel, because he, as an ordinary teenager, finds it exhausting to try and keep his stories straight. Which is why stress and tension are such close companions of his. And it hasn't got easier to keep this up the longer he's done it, but harder. He could teach your average spider a thing or two about weaving webs. At least he can eliminate undercover agent as a possible career choice. He wouldn't last a month.

Last week Orlando ran into one of his father's cop friends in Peakston, and his heart didn't just stop, it screeched to a halt and fell flat on its face. Orlando wasn't meant to be in Peakston. Not that Sergeant Lujd could possibly know that, but it wasn't the sergeant Orlando was worried about. Worst-case scenario: Orlando turns a corner and walks straight into his father. Less-worst-case scenario, but still bad enough: Sergeant Lujd inadvertently says something to Officer Gwinnet about seeing his boy the other afternoon way over in Peakston. Officer Gwinnet would be suspicious immediately, no matter how casual the remark. *Who were you seeing? What were you doing? What's going on? Why were you there?* Sergeant Lujd, for his part, seemed pretty happy to run into Orlando. Sergeant Lujd is looking forward to the coming basketball season, as is the rest of the force. Sergeant Lujd didn't say so, of course, but Orlando knows the officers bet amongst themselves. Sergeant Lujd told him (as he always tells him) how proud Orlando's father is of him – all of them are. Sergeant Lujd has three daughters, which, apparently, limits his chances of pride. "What are you doing so far from home?" asked Sergeant Lujd. Through the ice-sculpture smile that had formed on his face Orlando said he was doing an errand for his mother. Fortunately, the sergeant didn't ask him what that errand was; Orlando can't come up with more than one spontaneous excuse at a time.

Needless to say, there was no errand for his mother.

When basketball isn't on Orlando goes twice a week to a ballet class. He used to go once a week. His teacher was always trying to persuade him to increase his lessons, but it wasn't until the end of last year – after Sorrel dumped him – that Mrs Andonis succeeded in getting him to agree. He needed a new distraction. She lets him use one of the practice rooms without charge whenever he can fit it in. Basketball will be on soon, so he's making the most of this time, sneaking off to the studio whenever he can. His father thinks that he and Ruben hang out a lot, like they used to; still go on long hikes and camping trips. And that Orlando spends a lot of time playing friendlies with teammates and boys from nearby schools, getting in that extra practice Bernard Gwinnet values so much. God forbid he ever finds out the truth.

Orlando has been dancing since he was four, when his mother took him with her to pick up a friend's daughter from her class one rainy afternoon. He can't remember the friend's daughter or her name, but he remembers standing in the doorway with Suzanne, watching the twirling little girls, all of whom, in his memory, were dressed in silver, their hair tied up with ribbons of blue or green. They reminded him of dragonflies; light and graceful dragonflies. And he remembers thinking, *That's what I want to do.* (Not be a dragonfly or wear silver and coloured ribbons, but dance.)

By then his father was already complaining that Orlando was nothing like his brother Raylan – no manual dexterity, no coordination, no interest in any sport, not even as a spectator. "What's wrong with that boy?" his father would shout at his wife. "You mollycoddle him. You spoil him too much." Which was not something Bernard was likely to do. But, despite his father's best efforts – which included running Orlando around the block, making him do push-ups in the yard and forcing him to join teams where he was always left on the bench – Orlando never improved. Athletic as a potato, according to his father. "Throws like a girl and runs like a girl," declared Officer Gwinnet. Whereas Raylan ran like a boy as soon as he could walk, threw like a pro as soon as he could grip a rattle and was playing baseball at three and on a Mighty Mites football team by the time he was six. Raylan, the future sports legend, was still alive then, of course. And so Officer Gwinnet, not really paying much attention to his youngest son, allowed Orlando to attend Luanne's School of Dance, thinking that the lessons might build his muscles and improve his motor skills. Which they did.

Everything changed when Raylan died. Suzanne turned to Jesus for comfort; Bernard turned to Orlando. Orlando was seven. Suddenly, from being largely ignored by his father unless he was being criticized, he became the centre of his father's world, although not as he might have wanted. Now he was his father's last and only hope. Orlando wasn't a replacement for his brother – his father never tires of telling him how inferior he is to Raylan in every way – but his stand-in. Second best, he'll have to do. In his fixation on Raylan and his football career, Officer Gwinnet had forgotten all about the dance lessons, but now they were cancelled. "Time to get serious," he told Orlando. "Time to be a man." Meaning, time to be a basketball player (too slight for football, but tall). Orlando never thought about arguing or resisting, it's not the way things are done in the Gwinnet household. They might sneak around or crawl under, but they never confront head-on. It's not worth it. And so he fell in with Officer Gwinnet's plans for him. High-school basketball, then college basketball, then professional basketball. If that fails, he'll study IT or engineering, just as Raylan would have done. The fact that Orlando has no interest in basketball, IT or engineering is immaterial to his father. At least Raylan did love football.

Orlando, however, does have two parents. No one would ever describe Suzanne Gwinnet as feisty or confrontational, and fewer would mistake her for a feminist. She believes that since her husband pays the bills he gets to call the shots, and she defers to him in most things, which is just as well as her husband is a man who insists on getting his way – no matter how. But she has learned to live around him as much as she can – to use his preoccupation with himself and indifference to everything else to her advantage.

Understanding how much her surviving son loves dance, Suzanne eventually found another class for him, this one in Peakston, and enrolled Orlando under a different name so that, with any luck, there is no way this insubordination could ever get back to her husband.

And so Orlando's double life began. An aspiring Michael Jordan most of the time, a Carlos Acosta wannabe when no one (especially Officer Gwinnet) is looking. Not even Ruben knows about the ballet. It's not a secret if you tell anyone.

On this Thursday, Orlando parks nearly a mile away and slouches to the studio, sweatshirt hood up and head down, keeping close to buildings and taking the most circuitous route he can. Just in case he runs into someone he knows – it happened before, it can happen again. You only have to be shot once to be shy of guns.

Today, however, everyone he passes is a stranger. Nonetheless, when Orlando finally reaches his destination he feels as relieved as a soldier who's just made it through a minefield. Safe at last.

It seems he took an even more convoluted route than he thought, because when he opens the door to the Andonis Dance Studio he discovers that, for the first time since he started here, he's late. The other students are already warming up.

"There you are, Bryan!" calls Mrs Andonis. Mrs Andonis is owner and principal teacher of the studio. Bryan is the name Orlando's known by here; Bryan Grainger. Bethany Grainger is a friend of his mother; it is she who signs the cheques that pay his fees. "We were afraid you weren't coming." Of course she was. There used to be two boys in this class, but one moved.

"Sorry, Mrs Andonis," says Orlando. "I'll be ready in a couple of minutes."

He opens the door of the small room (or large closet) in which he and Mrs Andonis' assistant, Rios, change. And once again his heart slams on the brakes and falls over. If there was one advantage to seeing Sergeant Lujd last week, it is that it put seeing Sorrel dancing around his kitchen and giving his father the finger right out of his mind.

Which is where she has stayed. Until now. For here she is, sitting on the step stool in the corner, reading a book about the pioneering choreographer Katherine Dunham. As if Sorrel ever read books; as if she would ever have heard of Katherine Dunham. Sorrel's wearing black leggings and a black leotard, and has her hair scraped back in a tight bun. Her feet are bare, and so dirty she may have been walking the streets without shoes. As if Sorrel would ever be seen in public with dirty feet.

Orlando stands still for several seconds, gawping. He can't believe he managed to forget about her. Can't believe he convinced himself that she wouldn't be back. What a jerk. Here he was terrified about bumping into the sergeant again. If only. That's like worrying about a dripping tap when you're about to be hit by a tornado. At least Sergeant Lujd is alive, which has its own problems, of course, but not as many as Sorrel being dead has if you really think about it. It might occur to Orlando that he has just learned an important lesson – that people often focus on the wrong things in life – but it doesn't. All he can think of at the moment is how much he wishes she'd go away.

Sorrel, however, has no intention of going anywhere.

"God, what took you so long?" She shuts the book with a snap. "What'd you do? Walk here? You must know everybody was waiting for you. Like you're the guest of honour or something." She gives him a conspiratorial wink. "I bet they all have crushes on you. All those girls? Even the teacher. Mrs Andonis – that's her name,

yeah? The woman with the thin lips? She kept checking her phone and looking at the door, getting wound
up tighter than a screw lid you'd need the Terminator to
open. *Where is he? Why isn't he here?* She kind of reminded
me of my mom. Which is not really something a person
would want."

Mrs Andonis has never reminded Orlando of Meryl
Groober, not even for a split second. He likes Mrs Andonis.
Which can't be said about his feelings towards Sorrel's
mother, but that doesn't stop him feeling compelled to
defend her. "Okay, I get that your mom's a little controlling, but she—"

"A little controlling?" interrupts Sorrel. "You mean,
like your dad's a little controlling?"

Orlando can't even think about his father – never
mind name him out loud – just in case that makes him
appear. He opens his mouth and shuts it again.

"Not that I think Mrs A is really like the Groober,"
Sorrel babbles on. "It was just that she was so worked up.
You know, like the day was ruined because you weren't on
schedule. I'm sure she's way nicer than Meryl the Peril."
Sorrel laughs. Very briefly. "She'd pretty much have to
be, wouldn't she? Still, you can't really tell by looking at
someone, can you? I mean, if you think of all the hor-
rible things that happen in the world, who does them?

You don't see someone on the street and right away think, *Wow, I bet he beats his wife…* Or, *I bet she locks her kids in the closet…* Let's face it, most people are not half as good or cool or even sane as they act, are they? I mean, how many people would you really trust? If your life totally depended on them, who do you think you could count on?"

Is this what death does, makes you cynical? Critical? Suspicious? In his memory, Sorrel was always pretty sweet and easy-going. She could be sarcastic, but she wasn't mean. Even when she dumped him she was nice about it. There wasn't any fight, or big scene or recriminations. And they were still friends; nothing changed in any major way. Things, however, have changed now. He starts to say that there are quite a few people he trusts – at least two of them with his life – but she cuts him off. She used to let him speak.

"But she is real disciplined, your teacher, isn't she?" says Sorrel. "Dancers have to be super disciplined. Kind of like models, I guess. But more so. I mean, they do more than wear clothes, walk and turn, don't they? But if you're really ambitious… You know, ambitious so nothing else matters – not love or a gorgeous sunset or hearing a song that makes you smile – not even the thing that you're ambitious about. If you don't get any real joy from it, but you just want to win, then you lose perspective. And that can make you ruthless. Like your dad – he's ruthless, isn't he? Like my mom. She wanted to be a big-deal model, and your dad wanted to be a big-deal athlete."

Another of the great disappointments in his father's life, though he's not sure how Sorrel knows that. "You don't always get what you want," mutters Orlando, thinking of himself.

"But your dad sure is trying," says Sorrel. "He's making you one instead. You know, because your brother's dead. If your brother were still alive your dad probably wouldn't even notice you're there. Anyway, he's like my mom. Everything has to be the way they say. It's all about them. What if they had real power? Like if they ran a country or something? They'd be tyrants. Guaranteed. Do you think maybe they're related? People like that? Do you think there's a gene that makes them crazy mean? Hitler. That Kim Jong guy. My mom and your dad."

Is she really comparing Mrs Groober and Officer Gwinnet to the ex-dictator of Germany and the current dictator of North Korea?"

"I said *if* they had power like that. You don't have to be so defensive."

Now she's interrupting his thoughts. Did she always talk so much? He has no memory of that either. Not to him, anyway. She talked a lot to Celeste. The two of them were like a perpetual-motion machine of conversation. He used to wonder how they could possibly have so much to say to each other, hour after hour, day after day. But he didn't think she'd still be talking after she was laid in her grave.

"And your teacher calls you Bryan." Sorrel picks up where he didn't know she'd left off. "How come she calls you Bryan? Is that your middle name? Bryan? I never knew that. I've never heard anybody call you anything but Orlando." She gives him a waiting-for-an-explanation look. "Oh, I get it. It's a long story. And I can tell from your expression that you don't want to tell me what it is. Like you never told me about the ballet. You have more secrets than a cemetery. But that's okay." She shrugs. Graceful as a ghost. "Everybody has stories, don't they? And secrets. Gazillions of secrets. If secrets were water the whole planet would drown." She moves her shoulders in another spirit-gliding-through-a-wall gesture. "It's like we only think we know people, but we don't know them at all. All we see is the picture. You can't eat a picture of an apple, can you? But still we act like knowing the picture of someone is knowing them. That looking at a picture of an apple is the same as biting into it. Look at my brothers. I lived with them my whole tragically short life but I don't think I know them at all. I don't have a clue what goes on in their heads. Not that I'd want to.

I mean, duh. They're like doors you don't want to open because you're afraid of what's behind them. Anyway, if you put masks on them I'd never recognize them. When they're home they're always stoned and in their room. And when they're out of their room they're still stoned and don't have much to say. *Yes. No. Maybe. Tomorrow. Eat.* If they use sentences with more than two words it's because they want something." She giggles. Another trait he doesn't recollect. "You know what I call them? Tweedledumb and Tweedledumber."

When she dumped him, she refused to discuss it with him; she said there was nothing to say. Now she has so much to say she can barely get the words out fast enough. If she were real – and if he could squeeze some words into her monologue – he'd ask her how she knew where he'd be. Among other things. He'd ask her if Mrs Andonis knows she's here. He'd beg her not to tell his father – though even he knows that you'd only tell Sorrel something if you couldn't afford to take a full-page ad out in the papers. Which makes the fact that she isn't real good news. No worries about his father finding out because of her.

When at last she pauses (it can't be for air, neither ghosts nor hallucinations need air; maybe she's just tired of the sound of her own voice), Orlando says, "I know you're not really here, but I have to get changed."

She holds up her hands. "So go ahead. I'm not stopping you."

"I'd like a little privacy."

Her smile says she couldn't care less. "You think I never saw a guy in his underwear before?"

"I think I've never got dressed in front of a girl before."

But there is, of course, a first time for everything.

"Then you should try it. You might get to like it."

Orlando thought he was no longer mad at her for dumping him the way she did after that time in her room (a text message – the it's not you, it's me message – and a sad face), but apparently he is because he hears himself say, "Maybe you should've given me the chance when you were alive."

"And maybe I shouldn't have," says Sorrel.

He turns his back on her, gets into his practice clothes in record time and leaves the room without another glance. That'll show her.

Mrs Andonis begins the class by reminding them that today's the deadline for signing up for the auditions for the local drama group's musical production in the Spring. "It's a good cause," says Mrs Andonis. "All the proceeds go to help the homeless. But it won't be much of a production if they don't have any dancers." She looks right at Orlando. "And dancers need to be able to act."

"You should totally go in for that," says the girl on his right. Which is when he realizes that it's Sorrel.

He doesn't look over, but that, of course, doesn't discourage her.

"I bet you'd be good at acting. I figure you've had plenty of practice. But I don't know if you can sing. Can you sing? You know who has a great voice? Celeste. I know, you wouldn't expect it, would you? But she does. Only she's too self-conscious to sing anything except 'Happy Birthday' in front of anybody. She'll play the violin, the guitar and the piano to an audience, but she gets real nervous about singing. And she writes fantastic songs, but she's pretty shy about sharing them, too. But not you, you're not like that. You're used to an audience. And anyway, let's face it. You're never going to be a professional ballet dancer, are you? I know you know that. You can't put in the time. And anyway how would your father ever face the guys at the station? *My son, the ballerina.* Can you picture it?" She definitely does seem to have mastered giggling since she passed over, or under, or wherever it is she's gone. "I mean, seriously? But acting and dancing. That's different. Maybe he wouldn't like it, but it wouldn't give him a stroke. I really think you should consider it."

He continues to ignore her, concentrating on the clear, firm instructions of the thin-lipped Mrs Andonis. Sorrel's voice is like the sound of traffic or overhead planes or the burble of conversations happening around you, steady but unobtrusive.

Until she says, "She really likes you, doesn't she? Not my mom. My mom doesn't like anybody. She thinks she did like you. You know, because you're so good-looking and the big jock and everything. That's why she wanted us to go out together. I meant Mrs Andonis. She really likes you. You must be very good. That's what she thinks, isn't it?"

"Shut up," he whispers, and bumps into the girl on his left, who misses a step.

"You shut up," the girl whispers back.

"Like you're a natural," jabbers Sorrel. "You know, special. Not like me. I never had a talent for anything except looking good. If I'd been born ugly my mother probably would've had me adopted."

"Shut up," he repeats.

Mrs Andonis scowls in his direction. "Bryan! Focus!"

"I mean, I know you're pretty good at basketball but you really have to work at it, don't you? You have no magic. And probably you're only as good as you are because of the dancing. And you don't even like it really. I mean basketball, not dancing. The dancing you like more than anything. That's where your magic is. You're not going to get another life, you know. This is it. So why don't you do what you like?"

What he'd like to do is make Sorrel vanish.

"Bryan! Timing!" calls Mrs Andonis.

"I mean, I wish I'd done what I liked when I had the chance. Not that I knew what that was. I never really thought about it. I did my first commercial before I could even walk. And everybody thinks modelling's pretty cool. But maybe I would've liked to do something else. Only now I'll never know."

"Bryan! Hands!"

He has to make Sorrel shut up. Forgetting that she is either a phantasm or a figment of his imagination, Orlando comes down on her foot as hard as he can. He's lean, but he's solid muscle; if she were real he'd probably break it. It isn't Sorrel who screams. Of course.

Mrs Andonis stops the class. Serenity, the girl whose toe he's stomped on, is anything but. She howls, cries and collapses onto the floor. Orlando picks her up and carries her to a chair, apologizing over and over, "I'm so sorry. I don't know how that happened." It may be the pain, but although she assures him it's all right (through her tears) he isn't sure that she believes it was an accident. The bag of frozen peas that is kept in the office refrigerator for just such emergencies is brought out.

Once Serenity has calmed down and dried her eyes, and it's been established that nothing is broken, the class resumes – but this time there is no Sorrel beside him to nag and goad and get him into trouble.

All the while he's changing back into his street clothes, he's thinking about things Sorrel said. About his father. And her mother. What did she mean when she said that her mother wanted them to date? What did it have to do with her?

Mrs Andonis waylays him as he's leaving. "Bryan! Wait a minute!" She's smiling, so she must have forgiven him for stomping on poor Serenity's foot. "I just wanted to say how pleased I am that you decided to try out for the musical after all."

He did?

"I did?"

"Don't play coy." She holds up the sheet of paper headed *Peakston Players* that up until now was on the bulletin board in the hall. "You certainly did."

And there is his name, in a handwriting that even he would mistake for his.

Which makes this the moment when Orlando starts believing in ghosts.

18

Everyone's Patience Has Its Limits

~

October

Celeste sits on an uncomfortable chair, staring at the white walls of the dentist's waiting room and wondering if they've been painted that colour to encourage Dr Kostonapolis's patients to brush their teeth or if it was simply the cheapest paint they could find. Besides the uncomfortable chairs and white walls, there is a low table covered with free newspapers and old magazines (mainly women's). Besides Celeste, there are three other people waiting, all of them doing something on their phones. Because this is a Tuesday afternoon and both Ruben and Orlando are busy – and because she doesn't really have that many people to Snapchat, message on Tumblr, tweet or text any more – she has nothing to do but flick idly through the magazines. Celeste is not meant to be here. She is meant to be at orchestra practice. Which is where she'd very much like to be. This is the year she was really going to throw herself into her music so she wouldn't miss Sorrel so much, because music makes everything better, or at least bearable, but so far that plan isn't working out all that well. There is always something Astra has to do – a friend to visit, a club meeting to attend, a lesson to take – and it's usually Celeste who has to see that she does it. Lilah, as she gently, if constantly, reminds Celeste, is busy at the job that keeps the roof over their heads and a pack of hungry wolves from their door. She can't be expected to do everything. Last week Celeste missed orchestra because Astra lost her gym shoes and had to be taken to buy a new pair before the next class. The week before Celeste couldn't meet with her piano teacher because Lilah couldn't get away to take Astra to her tennis lesson. Sunday she missed the audition for the band that's looking for a guitarist because Astra had a fight with the friend she was visiting for the weekend and Celeste had to go and get her. Celeste can't refuse – only an ingrate would refuse such reasonable requests – and since going to yoga instead of having lunch with Iris Moon and her nephew, Celeste has been trying very hard not to be an ingrate. She also can't complain to her mother, because Lilah thinks music is "a nice hobby", but not something to be taken seriously (the way Celeste's father takes it). Celeste should be spending her free time on activities that will help her in the teaching career her mother has decided she should pursue (or that will help her get a boyfriend). It would be different if Celeste were missing Future Teachers of America meetings or some social event, those are things that do matter.

Celeste is here today on a coral-coloured plastic chair, staring at a heap of magazines that tell you what to wear, how to do your nails just like a professional salon and how to tell if your boyfriend's cheating – and not in the music studio tuning up with the rest of the orchestra – because, although the dentist is within walking distance, Astra can't be trusted to actually show up unless she's escorted. Astra is easily distracted by things she'd rather do; gym shoes aren't the only things she loses.

If only Sorrel were here. When Sorrel was alive, she often came along when Celeste had to do something with Astra. Sorrel's presence made everything easier. Easier for Celeste because it turned a chore into fun; easier for Astra because Sorrel was everything Astra wants to be so she was always trying to impress her, not destroy her will to live. Celeste puts down one magazine and picks up another (like cement blocks, they all seem very much the same).

If Sorrel were here, even as a ghost, Celeste wouldn't feel so cold inside. As if, no matter how high she turns up the heat or how many coats she puts on, she'll never feel warm. This isn't true, of course, and Celeste knows that. Eventually, she'll miss Sorrel less; she'll move on;

she'll make other friends, maybe even get the boyfriend or husband of her mother's dreams. Celeste will have her life with all the things that lives come with; Sorrel won't be in it, and, most of the time, Celeste won't even notice. But right now that eventuality seems very far away. So far away that it's easy to imagine it will never come. And, right now, Celeste is by herself, looking at pictures that remind her of Sorrel, like the last survivor of the village looking at the broken furniture and crockery that are all that remains. And wishing Sorrel had stayed at home that stormy night – or at least on the pavement; wishing she'd noticed her phone had gone AWOL sooner and hadn't missed Sorrel's call. Such a little thing to change the world.

She hears Astra's voice – the sweet and cheerful one she uses in public, especially with people who don't know her – saying goodbye to Dr Kostonapolis, and puts the magazine back on the table. Celeste pays with her mother's debit card (another issue of trust for Astra), while her sister sits in the nearest chair and redoes her lipstick.

Celeste would like to go straight home, but Astra can't possibly walk all that way until she's had a coffee. "I'm, like, totally shattered," says Astra. Celeste points out that all she's done this afternoon is sit in a chair and have her teeth cleaned. Astra says, "And?"

They take a window seat because Astra wants to see

and be seen should any of her friends pass by, although since she's on her phone the whole time a herd of bison could stampede past the café and she'd never notice. Celeste sips a small diet soda and takes out the book she's reading for school, but it's difficult to concentrate with all the noise, and with not wanting to be there in the first place. Astra has two cappuccinos (two sugars in each, Astra never puts on weight) while Celeste thinks of all the things she has to do after they get home, and counts the minutes slowly trudging by as if they're in chains.

When Astra is finally ready to leave, Celeste reminds her that they have to stop at the supermarket; their mother left a list.

"Not me," says Astra. "You know I hate grocery shopping." An activity she obviously believes her sister loves. "It's, like, so boring. I'm going home."

"We're supposed to stay together, remember?" Why did she give up her afternoon if Astra refuses to do what she's supposed to do? "Mom said—"

"Mom said you had to go to the dentist with me. She didn't say anything about what I had to do afterwards. And anyway I have homework for tomorrow. If I don't start it right away I won't get it done, and it'll be all your fault."

"I'm not the one who's supposed to do your

assignments," says the ever-reasonable Celeste.

"No, I am. You're the one who's trying to stop me. You want to tell Mom that?" Astra picks her bag from the floor with such force that it hits the table next to them. It's Celeste who says sorry. Astra says, "I'm going home."

Celeste does the shopping and is in the checkout queue behind a woman who can't find her wallet (*I know it's in here somewhere*) when her phone goes. Her sister's face beams back at her from the screen (one of the few times Celeste ever sees her smile). Should she answer it? There's no way Astra is calling to say hello. She wants something. Celeste starts to put the phone back in her pocket. But what if that's not why Astra's calling? What if something has happened? She could have had an accident. It wouldn't be the first time; or even the hundredth. Celeste answers the call. This time, fortunately, Astra didn't set anything on fire or flood the bathroom. Astra left her dirty gym kit in the café. "I guess I stuck it under the table and just forgot about it," says Astra. When Celeste says that Astra will have to go back for it (Celeste, after all, has the shopping to lug home) her sister starts to cry and shriek at the same time. *Nothing is fair … you're a selfish cow who only thinks of herself … it's too bad it was Sorrel hit by that car and not you…* When she finally calms down Astra says, "So you want me to call Mom and have her get it on her way home?" As this is something Lilah Redwing will definitely not want her to do, Celeste doesn't want it either. She goes back to the café and gets her sister's laundry, which is still under the table, sitting in a puddle. It is now rush hour in Beaconspoint. Celeste is waiting to cross a four-lane intersection, and trying (unsuccessfully) to keep Astra's bag from dripping on her, when two things happen at once: the light changes and her phone starts to ring. And keeps ringing, in a way that makes her think it is either an emergency or a mistake. She fishes it from her pocket as she steps into the road. This time it's her mother's face smiling back at her; it's an emergency. Because of the traffic and having her hands full, it's hard to hear what her mother is saying. "Mom? Mom? Are you okay?" *Something ... crisis ... something ... later ... something ... sorry ... something ... something ... supper.* There's a crisis at work so Lilah's going to be late and wants Celeste to cook. It's only when horns start honking and a car passes so close that it makes her jacket move that Celeste realizes she's standing in the middle of the road and the light is now against her – making it possible that Astra will get her wish after all. Drivers shout as they go by. *What the hell do you think you're doing? Get out of the f_____g road, you stupid girl! Are you completely nuts?* Someone throws an empty plastic bottle at her.

When Celeste arrives home she finds Astra stretched

out on the sofa, watching a movie and texting. A plate, a glass and a bottle of soda are scattered across the coffee table. "I thought you had homework," says Celeste. Astra ignores her. There is an opened loaf of bread, an opened jar of peanut butter and quite a few crumbs on the kitchen counter. It's as she's looking at the debris on the counter that Celeste starts shaking so much she has to sit down. She closes her eyes and feels the cars going by; hears the horns and *swoosh-whoosh* of tyres and people shouting out of their windows; imagines Sorrel's last seconds of life. Celeste has been her usual practical, competent self today. Unsinkable and unflappable. A very large and sturdy rock. It is when she remembers the plastic bottle bouncing off her head that the rock begins to crumble and the tears start to fall.

"There's no point crying now. It's all over." Sorrel laughs. "At least nobody mowed you down. You can be grateful for that. Where does the cereal go?"

Celeste opens her eyes.

Sorrel is standing by the counter with a box of cornflakes in her hand.

Celeste points. "Up there."

"Shouldn't Astra be doing this?" asks Sorrel. "You did the shopping."

Because asking Astra to do anything is

counterproductive (you spend half an hour nagging her and then do it yourself anyway), Celeste says, "She's busy."

"It's not like she's building shelters for the homeless," says Sorrel. "She's just warming up the couch."

Celeste wipes her eyes with the back of her hand. "I don't have the energy to fight with her right now. You know what she's like."

Sorrel makes an I-sure-do face. "You know what the problem with Astra is, don't you?" Sorrel opens the cupboard and slips the cornflakes onto a shelf. "She knows what *you're* like, that's the problem. You let her walk all over you."

"No I don't." Celeste says this with conviction, as if she doesn't know she's lying.

But Sorrel isn't fooled. "Oh, sure you don't. You're practically a human carpet, and you know it. You wait on Astra. You always let her have her own way. For God's sake, Cel, you even do her homework for her."

"Only when it's really hard."

"Oh, puh-lease... She's thirteen, not three." Sorrel sighs in a way Celeste doesn't remember her sighing before; as if she's a wooden bridge that is about to collapse. "If Astra murdered someone, you'd take the blame."

"No I wouldn't." She would; her mother would expect her to.

"And these?" Sorrel holds up two tins of beans in a questioning way.

"On the left."

Sorrel opens the cupboard on the left. She puts the beans on the shelf with the other tins. "You should've gone to your dad's in the Summer like he wanted."

"I couldn't. My mom—"

"Your mom would've acted like you'd stabbed her in the back if you'd gone to your dad's. Just like you'd be ripping out her heart if you turn out to be like him – and not like she wants you to be."

Celeste doesn't want to think that she and Sorrel ever argued, but they did, of course. And this is one they've had before.

"That's not what I was going to say. My mom wouldn't have been able to cope by herself." She can't expect Sorrel to understand. Sorrel was opposed to doing anything to help her mother or make her happy. The only reason she went along with the modelling was because she figured it would let her leave home faster. Maybe let them both leave. "She needs me."

Sorrel pretends to gag. "And what about you? What do you need?" She puts the milk and juice in the fridge. "You would've had a real vacation if you'd gone to Tylor's. He and Jake would've made sure of that. But oh no, not our Celeste. She can't do anything just for herself or because it's what she wants to do. She has to take care of everybody else."

"That's not true. I do plenty of things for myself."

Sorrel puts her elbows behind her on the counter, which makes her body look like a question mark. "Like what? Eat? Sleep? Brush your teeth? Because I don't notice you doing much. And nothing that Lilah doesn't approve of."

This is a dig; and another old argument.

Celeste rises to her own defence. "It wasn't that she wouldn't approve—" She breaks off when she sees the expression on Sorrel's face. She seems to have become something of a stickler for the truth.

"Give me a break, okay? Lilah doesn't approve of a music career. She wants you to be a teacher. So you're going to be a teacher. Lilah doesn't approve of same-sex relationships. She wants you to marry a doctor or a banker or some guy like that and be an important figure in your community. Is that what you're going to do, Celeste? You going to marry some guy because your mother wants you to?"

Celeste looks away. "I don't know. I— That's years away. I—"

"You don't know?" Sorrel crackles with indignation. "What do you mean, you don't know? You told me you wouldn't. You told me—"

"I know what I told you. And I meant it. But that was when you were alive." For all her wishing that Sorrel was with her earlier, she now wishes that she wasn't. Celeste may start crying again. "You're not here any more."

"I'm here now. But what matters is that you're here!" Suddenly Sorrel's sitting right beside her, leaning close. "You're here, Celeste. You don't need me to live the way you want. You just need you."

Celeste's voice is a mumble. "It's different now."

"No it isn't. You have to believe that. And you have to start doing things for yourself."

"But I do. I have my music. I do that for myself."

"Your music? You do your music for yourself?" Sorrel smirks. "Then why didn't you go to orchestra today? If you keep missing practice you're not going to be able to play in the big Christmas concert. And I bet if you talked to her, Ms Santos would give you a solo. You could do that song you wrote last year. Remember? About stars."

Of course she remembers. It was a present for Sorrel, that and the star earrings. "I love that song." She's hoping Sorrel will say that she loves it, too, but it isn't Sorrel who speaks next.

"Who are you talking to?" asks Astra.

"No one," says Celeste.

Which, of course, is now true.

19

If You Don't Succeed the First Time You Can Always Try Again

Ruben leaves his last class to find Orlando waiting in the hallway for him. Orlando's had an idea. Since it's such a beautiful day, why don't they take a hike along the river trail? They used to hike a lot together (they used to do a lot together, come to that), walking all day, sometimes camping overnight. It'd be like old times. But that, of course, was before. Before Ruben's mother got weird; before Orlando started giving ever more of himself to his secret life.

"What do you say?" Orlando fiddles with the strap on his book bag. "Practice'll be starting soon. I thought it'd be nice for us to have a little time together while we can."

"I don't know, man. I'd really like to." Ruben would really like to. He'd give anything to have the "before" time again – when he often didn't get back to Garibaldi Drive until it was time for supper, if not much later – even for a day. "But…"

"But what? You have to mop out the Augean stables before supper?"

Ruben winks. "Good guess."

"Come on. I'm not saying we should trek the Himalayas. Just a walk by the river. Just for an hour or two. We hardly ever hang out like we used to." Making it sound as if Ruben is the only one who's always busy. Orlando shifts his bag to his other shoulder, banging it against the wall in the process. "And, you know ... it hasn't exactly been a good year."

Tell me about it, thinks Ruben. And immediately feels bad. Orlando means because of Sorrel. First she breaks up with him, and then she dies. It's only now, watching Orlando pull at the strap of his bag, seeing the unhappy smile he's forced on his face, that Ruben realizes he's been so wound up in his own worries that he really hasn't stopped to think how Orlando must feel. On the other hand, how could he, when Ruben hardly knows how *he* feels from one day to the next?

"Oh, man, I really wish I could. I really do. But…"

But this is the after part, the "now". The days of self-absorption and let's-have-fun have gone the way of the raucous foosball and ping-pong tournaments, the late-night film marathons and Sylvia Rossi's famous lasagne dinners. Now he never loses track of time or forgets there was something he was meant to do; never does whatever he feels like on the spur of the moment. In the now, Ruben is arguably one of the most reliable and dependable teenagers in the Western world. He comes straight home unless he's told his mother he'll be late because he has something to do after school, and then he tells her exactly how late. He has no room for spontaneity.

"But I have a super full schedule this term. I'm out a lot of afternoons with extracurricular stuff. I really have to get home today. I promised my mom—"

Orlando nods. "Yeah, sure. I get it. I'm pretty overloaded, too. I just thought—"

Terrified that Orlando might suggest coming home with him instead, Ruben says, "Another time. Maybe next week." He punches him in the arm. "I'll see you tomorrow. We'll make a plan. I have to hurry." And starts to run down the hall. Even though running in the corridors is against school rules.

The truth is that even if Sylvia weren't expecting him, he wouldn't have gone for a walk, not even with the protection of Orlando. As if he's morphing into his mother, Ruben is spending even less time away from home. Inside the house is the only place he feels safe. Outside he's afraid Sorrel will appear again. The last thing his mother needs is for him to be picked up by the police for yelling at someone who isn't there. What if they decide that he's mad and send him away? How would she ever be able to cope with that? And the last thing he needs is to see Sorrel when he's with Orlando, someone who knows him so well. Ruben would never be able to hide it from Orlando if he saw Sorrel while they were together.

Ruben arrives home and steps inside, locking the front door behind him. He dumps his jacket and books on the sofa and takes the stairs two at a time. He's always anxious to make certain that Sylvia's there; and equally relieved that he is, too.

His mother is in her office, reading over what she wrote yesterday. She says her day, which, since she's still in her pyjamas, he guesses only started an hour or two ago, is going well. She's made some important changes, some significant decisions. She now realizes that Princess Mei can only escape the destruction of the city by pretending to be a boy. And that the great warrior Tatoka must risk being ostracized by betraying the king if he is to survive himself.

"What about Kia?" The mind is an amazing thing. Ruben may forget to pick up coffee or buy a birthday card for his uncle or where he put his keys, but he never forgets the details of whatever book his mother is working on at the moment. "Is she still locked in the dungeon?"

"She is," says Sylvia, "but you know how resilient she is. She's a fighter. She doesn't let things defeat her." Unlike some people. "She's going to find a way out soon. And then there'll be hell to pay."

His mother's novels are full of passion and destruction. Full of death and delusion; full of treachery and thwarted dreams. Which, he supposes, makes them fairly realistic. He's never actually read one himself, but he doesn't have to. She shares each chapter with him as it's written so that he knows each story by heart. She talks about her characters and what's happening in their lives the way she once talked about her family and friends. With enthusiasm and affection. With compassion and involvement. These days she's a lot more interested in the people of her imagination than she is in people of flesh and blood (even her own); possibly because they only die if she wants them to.

"I was thinking of adding a ghost," says Sylvia. "Sort of a spirit guide. What do you think? Do you think that's too far-fetched?"

She writes fantasy. Among many other things, there have been magic rings, shells, stones and daggers; monsters, demons and wizards; flying ships and disappearing mountains; talking animals and talking trees; fantastical creatures and fantastical worlds. What could she possibly mean by "far-fetched"?

"No," says Ruben. "Not at all."

Which he sees, as soon as he opens the door to his own room, was the right response. Not far-fetched in the least. Apparently, the Rossi house is no longer off limits. Sorrel is standing on a chair in front of his closet, rummaging through the boxes on the shelf over the clothes rail. Today she's wearing army fatigues and combat boots; she means business.

"Sorrel?" It isn't a question.

She doesn't turn around. "Hi, Ruben."

He wasn't expecting to find her in his room, but he also feels no real surprise. What he feels is a sense of acceptance (or, possibly, resignation). Which is an example (if an unusual one) of how adaptable humans are. A person really can get used to anything if they have to. Walking ten miles for water. Coping with deafness. Living in a windowless cell. Not eating meat. Sleeping in a doorway. Living with a visitor from the spirit world.

Because there's no one else in earshot, he can speak in a normal voice without any fear of being locked away. "What the hell do you think you're doing?"

"I'm looking for something."

In his closet? What could she possibly be looking for in his closet?

"What? No, never mind what. Get down from there."

She finally glances over her shoulder. Smirking. "Why? You afraid I'll fall and break my neck?"

"You're hilarious," says Ruben. "Now get down. You have no business going through my things."

"I'll get down if you tell me what's going on."

From his online research into paranormal experiences Ruben knows that most spirits are silent and remote – a figure walking the same path or hallway, or a face peering out of the same window or doorway at the same time every night. Not mouthy, interfering and keeping irregular hours.

"You want *me* to tell *you* what's going on? Excuse me, but I'm not the one who broke into your room. I'm not the one who shouldn't be here."

If he expected her to apologize, he has set himself up for another disappointment. She is now facing him, full on, one hand on the shelf and one on her hip – and is as apologetic as a tornado. "I didn't break in, Ruben. I walked in." He seems to be trying her patience. "You don't exactly have a padlock on the door."

As if that would do him any good.

"I didn't think I needed one. This is my personal space. I didn't invite you in, and now I'm asking you to leave."

"You don't have to invite me in. I'm not a vampire, I'm a ghost." She makes a face; he's being irritating and unreasonable. "And I'm not leaving until you tell me what's going on. I've looked all over and everything's gone. All your sketchbooks. All your canvases. Every last brush and piece of charcoal. I couldn't find even a crayon at the back of your desk."

Sorrel Groober, the spook that sleuths.

"That's why you're ransacking my room? You're looking for my art things?"

"What else would I be looking for? This isn't one of your mom's novels. There isn't any hidden treasure or a magic medallion or some warrior princess turned into a rock."

"Well you can stop right now. I got rid of everything. All gone. Nothing to find. Zilch. Nada. Cupboard bare. So get down."

"Really? Everything? I mean, I know you have this dumb idea to study business or law, but I didn't think that meant you were totally giving up art." She soundlessly jumps to the ground, standing so close he can tell she's not breathing. "If that's true, then, I think we need to talk."

"No, we don't." He steps back, putting an extra few inches between them. "What we need is for you to get out of here. I have stuff to do."

She steps forward, closing the gap. "So why did you dump everything? You were always sketching or painting something. Remember that watercolour you did of all of us trying to get Mrs Lancey's cat down from that tree?" Which was when they discovered that although a cat can climb a tree easily, getting back down can be a little more of a challenge. "Remember? Orlando's mom came running out with her phone and took the picture. And you turned it into a painting and gave us each a copy for Christmas? It was one of my favourite things ever. That and the one you did of me when I jumped in the lake." They were? Things he made were special to Sorrel? "But the one with the cat was the best. You got everybody perfect." She laughs, and it sounds the way sunshine feels.

He'd forgotten that day, forgotten the painting, but he remembers both of them now. It was a good day with a lot of laughter; and it was a good picture, Orlando standing on Ruben's shoulders, earnestly talking to Ruby, the cat, trying to calm her. Sorrel and Celeste holding on to each other, they were laughing so much. He has to wrench himself out of the memory. "I just lost interest, that's all." He shrugs. "It happens. You know. You grow up and you put away your toys."

"Toys?" This laugh is different, not sunshine but sleet. "What's that supposed to mean? We're not talking about a Star Wars lightsabre. We're talking about your heart and soul."

Since she obviously has no intention of moving away, he does, walking past her and sitting on the bed to take off his shoes.

"What about all your plans?" She follows and stands looking down at him. "You were going to travel all over, and live in houseboats and garrets and beach shacks. Remember? You were going to paint the world."

"Well, now I'm not." Now he's going to make money. Now he's going to have a private office with a big desk and a view of other buildings. Security gives you a pension; romance doesn't. "That was all kids' stuff."

"You're making a mistake," says Sorrel.

"So did you," says Ruben.

"Which one would that be?" she asks.

And immediately disappears.

At least she still has her sense of humour.

20

It's Usually Only His Father Who Tells Orlando What to Do

Orlando used to have a regular life. School, friends, family, work – going about his day just like everyone else, with the usual assortment of terrestrial experiences. Among which was the first sight he'd see when he opened his eyes in the morning – the painting Ruben did of the four of them getting Ruby out of the tree that hangs on the wall across from his bed – so that he also woke up with a smile. This morning the first thing Orlando sees is Sorrel sitting on the foot of his bed, blocking his view of the painting, messing around with his phone. Bizarre is the new normal. He isn't smiling now.

Orlando closes his eyes and counts to ten, but she is still there when he opens them again. "What do you think you're doing?"

"What do you think I'm doing? I'm waiting for a bus."

"What are you doing with my phone while you're waiting for your bus?"

"It's today." She doesn't look at him. "Obviously, it can't be left up to you, so I'm putting the details on here so you don't forget."

He has no idea what she's talking about, but he isn't going to ask. He doesn't want to encourage her – not that she needs any encouragement. She's become a real self-starter when it comes to haunting – her appearances so frequent that he's almost more surprised when he doesn't see her than when he does. He throws back the covers and gets out of bed. "Thanks."

"You forgot all about them, didn't you?" She's looking at him now. This is the first time she's ever reminded him of his father. "I knew you would. Even though you know how important the auditions are you totally deleted them from your mind."

So now he knows what she's talking about. "I didn't forget. That implies that I intended to go. But I didn't. That was never in my options menu." He pulls the cover back in place. "And maybe they're important to you, but they're not important to me. So don't waste your time putting the info on my phone."

"I'm not the one who's wasting their time." If it's possible, she may be slightly better at conveying disapproval with just a look than even Officer Gwinnet. "Because if you don't find something to do besides throw a ball through a hoop you're going to end up a miserable old man, giving off unhappiness the way you once gave off sweat."

"What are you now? The lifestyle guru from beyond the grave?"

"I'm your friend, that's who I am. I'm trying to help you."

"You're my dead friend, whose help I don't want or need. And I don't have time to try out for some stupid musical. The season's starting soon. I have practice this afternoon."

"The season doesn't need you to start. It'll start every year just like always long after you're dead," she informs him. "And, unlike basketball, this isn't a game. Your future's at stake."

"At least I have one," snaps Orlando.

This time she gives him the finger. "It's not going to work, Orlando. You're hoping that if you insult me and act like you don't care I'll just go away."

"Praying," said Orlando. "I'm praying you'll go away."

"What a difference a few months make." She gives him an almost seductive smile. "Remember when you didn't want me to go?" She flops down on her stomach, her chin on her hands. "*Please, Sorrel, please. Give me another chance.*"

Is it possible that she was always like this? Petty?

Antagonistic? Argumentative? Bossy? Wouldn't he have noticed?

"You're out of your mind, you know that?" He grabs his clothes and marches past her.

"I'm not the one who's crazy. That would be you, Gwinnet. As you keep pointing out, I'm the one who's dead." She follows him across the room, putting her face close to his. "So don't you remember when you wanted me around, Orlando? You forget that, too?"

If only he could. When Sorrel dumped him he started wondering if his father wasn't the only one who wished Orlando was someone else. That maybe everybody did. "I don't want to talk about that now. I have to get ready for school."

He leaves the room, shutting the door quietly but firmly, and can still clearly hear Sorrel say, "You wanted to talk about it then. I was the one who didn't want to discuss it."

He opens the door again and puts his head in. "Well, you waited too long to change your mind," says Orlando. This time he slams the door behind him.

He expects to find Sorrel in the kitchen with his mother when he goes down for breakfast (probably sitting in his chair to really annoy him), but, dispelling his fear about the shortage of mercy in the world, Suzanne is by herself, sipping a coffee and listening to the news on the radio. She smiles when he walks in. "How did you sleep, honey?" At least his mother loves him.

This is the year when everything fell apart. Things began going downhill last December. That was when Sorrel abruptly broke up with him (when he'd been thinking everything was going really well). Then Ruben (his brother in every sense except parents) suddenly turned into a human NO TRESPASSING sign. Then Celeste (always warm and open) became distant and guarded. Orlando's response was to intensify his life of subterfuge, paranoia and deceit. The four of them stumbled on like that until the Spring, when Sorrel was killed. As if the universe wanted to prove that things can always get worse. Which they have. Now, despite his popularity at school, his mother's prayers and his father's constant surveillance, Orlando feels alone. Where did everybody go? How did they wind up here? If this year were a sports team, it would be one organized in Hell from the worst sinners throughout human history, the Devil himself as coach and his closest henchmen jumping up and down in the bleachers, throwing off sparks and sulphur and shrieking: "Don't let them get the ball!" That's why he had the idea to have a walk with Ruben before practice started. To snatch a couple of hours of normality from the jaws of chaos. He should have known that wouldn't work. Because Ruben, as usual, was busy. Had to rush home. Was sorry, really sorry. He'd see him tomorrow; they'd set something up. But, as often happens, tomorrow never came. Not that one at any rate.

Although Orlando doesn't want to be the basketball star his father is determined he'll be, he wants to be normal; to belong. Which is why, as he walks towards the gym this afternoon for the first pre-season practice, he's in a better mood than he's been in all day. If there's one thing that can get Sorrel out of his mind, this is that one thing. His heart may not be in basketball, but he enjoys playing. Back with the boys. Cooperation. Camaraderie. Guys fooling around. Everything okay. When you're on a team, you automatically belong.

It's all *Go, Beacons! Go!* when he gets to the gym. The locker room is buzzing with energy and anticipation. Positivity. The drive of competition. This year, says Coach Mena, they're going to be state champions. They have to be. It's what they've worked so hard for every season. It's in the bag (or in the basket). There'll be no slacking, no half-heartedness. He doesn't want them to try hard, he wants them to win. It isn't how you play the game, it's whether or not you lose.

But as soon as they hit the court, Orlando's enthusiasm

starts to falter. He finds it difficult to concentrate. He thinks he sees Sorrel sitting on the bleachers and drops the ball. He glances over to make sure the person standing in the doorway isn't Sorrel (it isn't) and gets hit with the ball. He imagines her showing up at a game and trips over his own feet. He wonders if she's going to be waiting for him when he gets home, the way she sometimes is, and slams right into Jenner Loudon, bringing them both down.

"You played like shit, Gwinnet," Coach Mena tells him when it's over – just in case he hadn't noticed. "I hope it's because you have a raging fever and are slightly delirious."

"I do think I'm coming down with something," Orlando mumbled. "I'll be okay next time."

His father's working nights this month, but even so Orlando isn't ready to go home. He gets in the car and starts to drive. He's paying no attention to where he's going or how long it's taking him to get there. He just wants to shake off the defeat of the afternoon; to get rid of the guilt. He's stopped at a light when he sees, across the street, the old church that's been turned into a community centre. The Parsons Lane Community Centre. He's come all the way to Peakston without even noticing. He pulls out his phone and goes to contacts. Of course, that's where the drama club meets, where they're holding auditions. But he's not trying out for a part; he's not going in. On the other hand, because he never told Mrs Andonis to take his name off the sign-up sheet, and never told the club he wasn't coming, they'll be expecting him. Orlando is experienced at feeling guilty, and now he feels guilty about not being brave enough to say right from the start that he wasn't going to try out for the play. And guilty about letting them think that he was. He pulls into the car park.

The director is a small, intense woman named Stella Brood who doesn't give the impression that she puts up with much nonsense, and definitely not for long. Stella Brood is very glad to see him. "You're on my list," she says, showing him her list. "I can't tell you how glad I am to see you. I was starting to think you'd changed your mind."

"Not exactly," says Orlando. "But the thing is, I only came to tell you that I can't try out or anything. I can't be in the play after all. I mean, even if you wanted me."

"Why wouldn't I want you?" She has to look up at him, but he somehow feels as if she's looking down. "Talented dancers aren't exactly crowding the streets around here." She nods, agreeing with herself. "And Mrs Andonis says you're very talented. I just need to see if you do more than dance."

"Yeah, well…" He shrugs. "I don't know about that.

But even if..." And Orlando explains about basketball season. November to February. Practice just started and happens almost every day. It would be impossible for him to fit in rehearsals. She could never rely on him. And then there are the games themselves.

"I don't see any problem," says Stella Brood. "We're very flexible. Most of our cast and crew have day jobs so we have to squeeze in our sessions when we can. Besides—" she pats his hand— "Our production isn't until April. That gives you plenty of opportunity to make up for lost time."

When he gets back to the car, Sorrel is sitting in the passenger seat, filing her nails.

He pretends he doesn't see her. He gets in and starts the engine.

"Well?" she asks as they turn onto the road. "Aren't you going to thank me for making sure you didn't miss this opportunity?"

"No," says Orlando. "No, I'm not."

"You didn't use to be so grumpy," says Sorrel.

She leans over and hits the horn. Then disappears.

21

Cinderella Redwing

~

November

The Redwing house is peaceful at the moment – making it a moment to savour and cherish. Astra is in her and Celeste's room with Winnie. Lilah isn't home yet. Celeste is in the kitchen. On the table is a pile of college catalogues that Celeste is determined to go through tonight (again), in order to finally decide where she's going to apply. Right now, however, she is fixing supper because Lilah is going to get home late, which, of course, is less unusual than if she were going to be early or even on time. Lilah probably has one of her groups after work, though Celeste doesn't know which one. It could be her Spanish lessons. It could be jive dancing or her book club. It could be her exercise class or Pilates. It could be just about anything really. Lilah has been a collector of learning since her divorce, dabbling in this and sticking her toe in that. In one class and out the other, as her ex-husband often says. Jill of all trades and mistress of none, which he also often says (though not to her). The ultimate groupie, Sorrel used to say.

That is not, however, what Sorrel says now as Celeste opens the oven door and slides the casserole she's made inside.

"Cinderelly … Cinderelly … scrape the dishes … do my wishes … scrub the floors … and wash the doors…" chants Sorrel, waving a wooden spoon as if it's a conductor's baton. "Clean the crisper … feed your sister … do it faster … you're no master … Cinderelly … Cinderelly…"

Celeste looks around to see Sorrel sitting with her legs folded under her on the work island, where she wasn't sitting two minutes ago. "You're not funny," says Celeste.

"Oh, but I think I am," says Sorrel. "I think I should have my own show. *Out of this World*. How's that for an attention-grabbing name? I bet the ratings would go through the stratosphere. I'd be on the cover of every magazine in the world. Only I'm not sure I photograph too well."

This time Celeste laughs. "Okay, you're a little funny. But only sometimes."

Not that long ago, when she thought she'd never see Sorrel again, Celeste sometimes felt that she might not be able to survive the loneliness. And that, never likely to hear another Sorrel Groober wisecrack, she might never laugh again either. But those things no longer worry

Celeste. Now Sorrel has started visiting almost as frequently as she did when she was alive. Sometimes Sorrel is silent and distant – sitting beside the unsuspecting Astra, watching a film, riding in the back seat of the car with them, looking out of the window as they come up the drive, watching Celeste rake leaves from her seat on the porch. But at other times, she's talkative and warm – lying on Celeste's bed with her, sitting beside her on the sofa, walking next to her on the street – full of gossip and opinions and ideas, just like before she died.

This is, clearly, a talking visit, but Celeste isn't sure she's in the mood to listen. Not tonight. Lately Celeste's conciliatory and look-on-the-bright-side nature has been experiencing some dark patches, and tonight seems to be one of them. She doesn't want to be cooking supper; she doesn't want to be dealing with Astra and Winnie; she doesn't want to be choosing a college from among her mother's suggestions, Lilah's favourites flagged on important pages with bright orange sticky notes. And she doesn't want to be hearing what's wrong with her from Sorrel, who is nothing if not direct. At least when Lilah tells Celeste what to do she says things like, "Are you sure that's what you want?" or "Do you think that's right?" or, "Oh, really? Well, if you think so…" – making it sound as if she isn't criticizing her at all.

"I'm not trying to be funny." Sorrel taps the spoon against the utensil pot. "I've been watching you since you got home from school." In that time, Celeste has done the breakfast dishes, put on a load of washing, done damage control in the bathroom after Hurricane Astra's morning passage, cleaned up the mess after Astra and Winnie made themselves a snack (how do you get peanut butter on the ceiling unless you deliberately throw it there?), found her sister's favourite jumper (the loss of which was likely to bring about the end of the world), put the washing in the dryer, replaced the burnt-out light bulbs in Lilah's room and in the hall (a skill that only Celeste possesses) and, of course, made supper. "I'm trying to make a serious point."

Celeste opens the fridge and takes out the salad things. "What point is that? That you're a fan of Disney movies?"

"My point is that you're like Cinderella. *Do this. Do that. Hurry up. Do it faster.* Cinderella Redwing. The unhired help."

Sorrel hid it well when she was alive, with her pretty-girl looks and sunny personality and her extensive knowledge of fashion and celebrity culture, but there was always a streak of rebellion in her. She pretended to conform, but secretly she was waiting for the time when she was out of school and out of her family's home and free. And now she is free. Free to eat chocolate cake, wear whatever she feels like and say whatever she's thinking.

"No I'm not." Celeste says this quickly. And then, although she doesn't mean to, adds, "Cinderella's beautiful. I'm more like one of the ugly stepsisters."

"No you aren't." Sorrel aims the spoon at her. "First of all, the ugly stepsisters did diddly squat. Second of all, you know I think you're beautiful."

Celeste's answer is to turn on the tap and start washing the tomatoes in a careful, get-those-pesticides-off sort of way.

"And besides," Sorrel continues, "beautiful is as beautiful does." She puts the spoon back in the pot. "If Astra looked the way she acts she wouldn't win a beauty contest against a bunch of blobfish."

That comment does get a response. "I thought you liked Astra."

"Did you?" Sorrel's voice is a yawn. "I never thought you did."

"What's that mean?" Celeste drops the tomatoes into the sink and looks around, the water still running. "Of course I like her. I love her. She's my sister."

"Sister blister. She's a pain in the ass, and you know it. A selfish, lazy pain in the ass."

"No she isn't." Celeste turns off the tap. "She's very sensitive. You don't understand how much the divorce upset her. She's never really recovered. You have to try and imagine. Dad was in her life one minute, and gone from it the next. He broke her heart."

"Oh please… Tylor didn't leave Astra, he left your mother. In fact, technically, he didn't leave, he was pushed. And he'd be in both your lives a lot more if Lilah would stop punishing him and let him. If anyone's breaking hearts around here, it isn't Tylor."

"You don't get it." Celeste takes the salad spinner from the cupboard and slaps it on the counter. "You can't expect my mother to just act like nothing happened. Not after what he did."

Sorrel balances on her arms, her feet folded in front of her; she was always a bit of a show-off in yoga. "What are we talking about now? What is it he did? You mean not wanting to work in a bank any more and quitting to have more time to do his music and have a life? Letting your mom kick him out because she wanted him to have a 'real' job and he refused to obey? Or falling in love with a man?"

Celeste starts ripping leaves off the head of lettuce and tossing them into the spinner. "Everything. He was married with children. He had responsibilities."

"Can you hear yourself?" Sorrel swings her legs to the left in Side Crow. She looks like a bird with a lot of questions. "You sound just like Lilah."

Celeste does, in fact, sound just like her mother. Probably because it is her mother who is always telling her how sensitive and unrecovered from the divorce Astra is, and how badly Tylor treated them, and how devastating it is to marry someone you think is interested in women and making money only to discover that neither of those things is true.

"No I don't." She turns the tap on again, pouring water over the lettuce.

"Oh, yes you do. For one thing, when has your dad ever shirked his responsibilities? He pays the mortgage. He pays child support. He bought your guitar and your keyboard. He pays for your music lessons. You really can't expect him to visit all the time, since your mother won't let him in the house."

The only reply from Celeste is the whirring of the spinner.

"Admit it, Cel," says Sorrel. "You act like you believe everything Lilah tells you. If she told you the moon was made of cheese, you'd try to eat it, just to please her."

"No I wouldn't." Celeste takes the tomatoes from the sink and puts them on the chopping board. "I know she's—" Several words come to Celeste's mind, but she doesn't want to say any of them out loud. "Not always right about things."

"Oh, I know you know that. But you'd never say that to her. You act like the only way of looking at things is Lilah's."

"That's ridiculous. I do have a mind of my own."

"Do you? Then what about all this?" Moving like air, Sorrel is now at the table, shuffling through the catalogues. "Why are all these colleges around here? Have they closed down all the ones more than a hundred miles away?"

Celeste starts to say that it's because those are the schools her mother says have the best teaching programmes, but amends it to, "Because they have really good teaching programmes."

"But you don't want to be a teacher," says Sorrel.

"It's a good career. It's something you can always fall back on."

"Or never crawl out of." Sorrel throws a catalogue at her. "And anyway, if you don't want to do it, it isn't a good career. A good career is the thing you love. You want to be a musician. Remember? Remember our plans?"

"Most musicians don't make enough money to feed a cat, and you know it. That's why it's more a hobby than a career," says Celeste, repeating something else her mother has told her more than once. "Besides, that stuff about being a musician was when you were alive.

Remember that?"

Sorrel groans. "Have I missed something? You keep forgetting that you're still alive, Celeste. And even if you want to have a back-up in case you're one of the millions of musicians whose cat dies of starvation, you could still live in the city, so you could go to college and do music at the same time. It doesn't have to be either or." She sails another catalogue in Celeste's direction. "You can't tell me they don't have any good teaching programmes in New York. And then you could live with your dad, and play in a band or whatever in your spare time. He doesn't think music's a hobby."

Celeste's mouth looks like heels dug into the ground. "You know I couldn't do that."

"Why not?"

Guilt. Resentment. Betrayal. Rage. The crippling migraines it would give her mother.

"My mom needs me to be nearby. She depends on me. She has nobody else."

"What you mean is that if she had to replace you she'd need a dogsbody, two maids, a cook and a nanny. Or do it herself." Suddenly Sorrel is standing right beside her. "All she has to do is tug on your strings and you do whatever she wants. She lets Astra act like a deranged prima donna, but she treats you like a servant."

"You don't understand." Celeste slips a knife from the block. "It's not easy being a single mother, Sorrel. It's really hard. She has to have a job *and* do everything at home."

"It looks to me like you're the one who does everything at home. And like you're going to keep doing it."

Celeste takes a knife to a tomato like an Aztec priest about to cut out a still-beating heart. "At least my mother cooks a meal now and then, which is more than your mother ever does."

There are things they've always known about each other – known and understood – but never really talked about. Until now.

"And at least my mother stays home now and then. Your mother isn't here even when she is. She's looking for dates online or reading one of her self-improvement books or talking on the phone. Or she's lying in the dark in case she's about to get one of her headaches."

Ignoring everything Sorrel just said about Lilah (all of which is true), Celeste says, "Why would you even want your mother home? All you ever did was argue. It's a miracle none of your neighbours ever called the cops." If Celeste could hear herself she would be shocked and embarrassed by how angry and mean she sounds. But she isn't listening, the words are just pouring out. "And you think my mom pulls my strings? Your mother never let

220

up on you for a minute. She was always on your case." Celeste stares at the knife in her hand. Where is all this coming from? Why? She has no idea, but she's powerless to stop it. As if she's opened the box that should never be opened and now can't put anything back. *Sit up straight. Brush your hair. Wear blue. Don't eat that. Maybe we should do something about your nose.* I know she was supposed to be your agent or whatever but it was more like you were the prisoner and she was the warden."

"I know that!" Sorrel screams back. "That's why we were always arguing! But I'm dead, so none of that matters any more. You matter. Do you know how much you've changed in just a few months? What happened to all our plans? We were going to move to New York or LA, and we'd share an apartment and I'd do my modelling and you'd do your music and—"

"And then you died!" Celeste throws the knife in the sink, tomato juice splashing against the tiles. "I'm not what's changed. It's everything else!"

"For God's sake, Cel, you can still have a life. You can still do everything we talked about."

"No, I can't. It's all different now. You died and ruined everything."

"It was an accident. You know that. I was so upset and calling you and not looking where I was going. But you know I couldn't take it any more. I had to tell her. Maybe if you hadn't been so afraid and we'd done it together— but oh no, you hate anything unpleasant or difficult, don't you? God forbid you should upset anybody." She steps even closer. "Or that anybody should upset you."

"I said I was sorry," shrieks Celeste. "What more could I do? I couldn't handle it. I thought you agreed we could wait till we finished high school. I said I was sorry!" She turns to march out of the room – and freezes.

Her mother has come home on time after all, and is standing in the doorway, Astra and Winnie behind her, eyes wide and mouths open. All three of them look as if they're the ones seeing apparitions.

"Celeste? Are you all right? What on Earth is going on?"

"I told you," screams Astra. "Didn't I tell you she's always talking to herself? Didn't I tell you she's, like, totally nuts?"

Winnie starts doing her impersonation of a hyena, hanging on to Astra to stop herself falling over with laughter.

Still standing beside Celeste, Sorrel smirks. "Let's see you get out of this one. Let's see you make this go away."

22

We Have to Talk About
Your Mother

Ruben used to fantasize about Sorrel. A lot. And when
he was asleep and couldn't fantasize, he dreamed about
her; dreams that had him waking sweating and tangled in
the covers or wrapped around his pillow. Once, in a dream
where he jumped from a cliff to rescue her, it was falling out
of bed that woke him. Many of Ruben's fantasies and dreams
incorporated things from his mother's novels, which are, of
course, the books with which he's most familiar – as well
as more or less being the world in which he lives when he's
at home. Sorceresses and wizards. Creatures of legend and
beings of magic. Ageless villains and timeless quests. Myth
over matter. The dreams and fantasies, like his mother's
books, often took place in impenetrable forests, on remote
mountains, on wind-blown deserts or in the underground
hideouts of gold-hearted bandits.

Right now, because the window is covered in a space
blanket and there is, of course, no electricity allowed in

here – and if you ignore solid but mundane objects like the sink and the toilet – it is possible to mistake the Rossis' bathroom for the cave of the warrior prince in Gaia Pendragon's novel *The Devil's Love* (Book Two in the Moondancer series). Close and dark and foggy with steam, the only illumination comes from the dozen tea lights whose tiny flames flicker in the gloom. The only sounds are running water and the melodious voice of a young woman telling stories in the night. The scent of lilac perfumes the air. But the running water is not an underground stream, it's the shower; and the sweet voice doesn't belong to the Earth guardian Chukona but to the phantasm Sorrel Groober. The scent of lilac also belongs to her.

Sorrel sits cross-legged on the lidded wicker laundry basket, talking – and Ruben stands under the shower, trying not to listen, wishing with all his heart that she would disappear for good. Once again, an event that a year ago would have been a dream come true – Sorrel Groober locked in a small, candlelit room with him – is now a nightmare.

Nightmare on Garibaldi Drive. From sexual fantasy to horror story in twelve short months.

"At least now I finally know why you wouldn't let me in that time. Remember? In the Spring? When I wanted to use the bathroom? You did everything but throw yourself across the front door so I couldn't get in the house."

"Sorry," Ruben yells back from inside the safe-zone made by the bath screen. "It's hard to hear with the water running."

"No it isn't. Not to hear me." And she's right, of course. Being dead, Sorrel is one person who doesn't have to shout to be audible over running water. He has no doubt that her voice would carry if he were standing under Niagara Falls. "So anyway, you know what's funny? We all knew we were banned from your house for some weird reason. But nobody could figure it out. Not even Orlando. I mean, we couldn't all have done something to piss you off. So it had to be that you were hiding something from us. That's why I wanted to come in, to see what it was. Anyway, even though I knew that none of us was allowed in, part of me thought the reason you were so determined not to let me in that day was because you were afraid to be alone with me." He sees her as a shadow through the glass of the screen, the ghost of a ghost. "You know, in case you couldn't control yourself."

Ruben's so surprised by this remark that he drops the flannel. She knew he had a crush on her? How could she possibly know that? He's the only person who knows that, and he never told anyone – especially not Sorrel.

"But I was way off on that one. Talk about making assumptions. Ego really blinds you, doesn't it? Like you believe you really are the centre of the universe and not just some cosmic debris in human form. It was because of your mom, that's why. You didn't want anyone to find out about Sylvia."

Thank God he's already squatting to retrieve the cloth or he might fall. And then, ridiculous as it is – because, obviously, since she comes and goes as she wants and apparently can walk through walls it's fairly difficult to keep anything a secret from her – says, "Find out what?"

"You can't be serious." Sorrel groans in a very un-spirit-like way. "We're not going to play more games, are we? First the I-can't-hear-you game and now the I-don't-know-what's-going-on-in-my-own-home game? Give me some credit, Ruben. I'm not exactly stupid. I mean, I know it's dark in your house, but I'm pretty sure you've noticed that your mom has a couple of issues. Like the agoraphobia and the electrophobia and all the rest of them. She's practically a human encyclopedia of phobias."

Ruben doesn't really want to talk about his mother. Not now, not ever. But especially not now.

"She's a writer." Usually he considers taking showers by candlelight as something of a hardship. It can be tricky if you lose track of the soap or misremember where you put the shampoo. He sometimes gets out and grabs his pyjamas or clean shirt instead of a towel. Tonight, however, he considers the poor visibility a godsend. If he can't really see Sorrel, then she can't really see him. Especially if he's crouched on the floor of the tub. "She's sensitive."

"Sensitive is having to wear a hat when you go out in the sun. Not covering your windows with foil."

"It's not foil, it's space blankets," he corrects.

"Oh, sor-reee… Blankets. Sheets. Stickers. What are you now, Professor Rossi? Every word has to be the exact right one? What's the difference? A sheet of foil by any other name is still a sheet of foil. What I want to know is why you didn't want me to know what's going on. Did you think I'd make fun of her?"

"No. Of course not." That actually hadn't occurred to him; Sorrel wasn't like that. It was the rest of the world he wasn't so sure of.

"Oh, I get it. You figured I'd blab."

She was like that. You had more chance of keeping a goat safe by putting it in the cage with a wolf than of keeping a secret safe by sharing it with Sorrel.

"That's not it." And here he is hunkered down in the shower, lying to someone who isn't really there. At least he sincerely hopes that she's not there. How can this be his life? "I just thought the best way to keep something private is not to tell anyone."

"Well, for your information, I happen to be very good

at keeping secrets. I've had plenty of secrets myself. But I can't believe you wouldn't tell Orlando. I mean, seriously? You think he would do anything to hurt you or your mom? And anyway, I would never drop your mom in it like that. Especially when she's had such a shitty time. Plus she's so nice."

At last, something they can agree on.

"Yeah," he says, "she is. She's real nice."

"That's why we have to talk," says Sorrel. "Just what are you planning to do about her?"

"I'm planning to have a cup of tea with her before I turn in."

"You know what I mean. She needs help. She can't go on like this, and you can't either. It's ridiculous."

"I do help her. What's ridiculous is you sitting out there so I can't finish my shower and get some clothes on."

"You think you're helping, but you're not. You're part of the problem, not part of the solution. And I'm not going anywhere. We need to have a serious discussion about Sylvia. She breaks my heart."

So that makes two things they can agree on.

"No we don't have to discuss her. My mom's fine, and I'm fine and everything's fine."

"Fine? You call this fine? Your mom barely comes out of her room. She won't turn on a light or pick up a phone.

She has no friends any more. And you're not much better. I worry about you, too. You think you're being positive, but what you're doing is giving up. Running away from life. You come out in daylight, but that's about it. You've pulled away from everybody, even Orlando. And you must know he needs you as much as you need him. His life's not exactly a vat of ice cream. Celeste's isn't either. At least Sylvia has her writing. But you – you've not only ditched your friends, you've ditched your painting, too. Do you really think that if you get some job where you make a lot of money, it'll protect you from bad things happening? How is that meant to work? You know what you're going to end up with? You're going to end up with nothing."

"What?" he shouts. "I think I got some water in my ear. Did you say something?"

He sees her move, coming closer. "You know, you're going to have to come out sometime, Ruben. If you stay in there much longer, you'll start to shrink."

He probably already has. He's been in here a while. He'd only just slid the bath screen shut and turned on the shower when Sorrel materialized. Since then, he's scrubbed himself twice, washed his hair twice and begged her several times to go away. Now she's peering through the opaque glass. Can she see him? Will she walk through it?

"I'll come out when you leave," he yells.

"For God's sake, Ruben. I want to talk to you, not look at you."

"What'd I say, Sorrel? I'll come out when you leave."

"Really? You're going all modest on me?" If he were in one of his mother's books, her laugh would be the warning sound of a Grenoch. "What are you worried about? I thought you don't believe in ghosts."

So did he.

"That's the deal, Sorrel. If you don't go, I'll stay in here till I shrink so much I go down the drain and then you won't be able to harass me any—"

Suddenly there's a banging on the bathroom door. A frantic banging. "Ruben? Ruben?" The doorknob rattles desperately. "Ruben? Are you all right? Who are you screaming at? Are you okay?"

Damn it. Was he making that much noise? This is all he needs.

"I'm fine, Mom. I'm fine." If he wasn't screaming before, he certainly is screaming now. "I'm just finishing up."

"Is there someone in there with you? Who's in there with you? Should I call the police?"

"No! No!" Terrific. She must be scared out of her mind if she's willing to pick up the phone. "Don't call the cops. I'm fine. I was just… I'll be right out."

He turns off the shower, grabs the towel from the

rack behind him, wraps it around him and slides back the glass. Given the way she fades in and out like a faulty light, he doesn't expect Sorrel still to be there, but of course she is. She has made it her mission to make his life even worse than it already is. She's sitting on the sink now, looking as serene as the little red Buddha in Bread and Land.

Although Ruben isn't a boy given to dramatic gestures, he yanks open the bathroom door, planning to storm from the room. And nearly collides with his mother, standing there with a lantern in her hand and all the worries of the world in her face. He never yells at her, but he yells at her now. "Christ, Mom, I have to get dressed!"

As he strides away he hears Sorrel say, "This isn't over, Ruben."

Of course is isn't. She has all the time in the world.

23

Black Friday, Bordering on Grey

It's the day after Thanksgiving – the day when, having just celebrated all they're grateful for, people flock to the nearest shopping centre or mall to buy more things to inspire their gratitude – and Lilah has taken Astra and Winnie shopping. Celeste has stayed home by herself. This time Lilah didn't try to persuade her to come or argue that Celeste spends too much time on her own. Ever since Lilah found Celeste shouting in the kitchen, she's been treating her with the careful good cheer you might show to someone who has no idea how ill she is. No subtle nagging. No I'm-only-thinking-of-you pep talks. No wouldn't-it-be-fun pressure for Celeste to have a party, or at least go to one. No I'm-sure-I-told-you surprise guests with young men in tow. Lilah even turned down two Thanksgiving invitations to dinners that included several male members under twenty, instead making a meal for just the three of them and leaving the room when Tylor called.

And, although neither of them said sorry, things between Celeste and Sorrel quickly returned to normal – or what passes for normal when your best friend's a ghost. The night after their fight, Celeste woke up as Sorrel slipped into bed beside her, whispering, "I promise I don't snore any more." It was the best Celeste has slept since June.

At the moment, she's killing time until Ms Santos picks her up to take her to an orchestra rehearsal. Celeste (as predicted by Sorrel) has a solo in the upcoming concert, performing the song she wrote last year, and is also playing a set with The Blues Cousins, whose lead guitarist has one arm in a cast until the new year. While she waits, she and Sorrel sit on her bed, watching videos of Tylor Redwing and his band Timequake on YouTube.

"I can't believe you never showed me any of these before." Sorrel's head sways to the music. "They're really good. I mean like really good. No wonder he didn't want to work in a bank."

Celeste beams. "I told you they're terrific."

"So is this song they're doing now an original or a cover?"

"My dad wrote it." Her voice beams, too. "He writes all their songs."

"Of course," says Sorrel. "I should've known. That's

where you get your talent from. He must be really proud of you."

"I guess." Celeste's voice loses some of its shine. "I mean, he is – but he hasn't really heard me play. Not live. Just on a couple of videos I've sent him."

"Really? Never? That's kind of grim." Sorrel looks over. "Hey, I know. Why don't you invite him to the Christmas concert? I bet he'd love to come."

As it happens, this is an idea that has passed through Celeste's mind more than once in the past couple of months. Sorrel's right, of course: her father would love to come. And because she knows how much he'd love it – although she talks to him about the orchestra – she never mentions the concert.

"So?" prompts Sorrel. "Why don't you ask him? It's a terrific idea."

Celeste sighs. "You're just saying that because it's your idea."

"No, I'm saying it because it is a really good idea. You know it is. It has to matter to you what your dad thinks of your music. You know, since he's so good himself." And, looking back at the screen, adds, "And since he cares."

Of course it's a good idea. It makes sense. Why shouldn't Tylor be there? He's not just her father, he's a fellow musician, too. On both counts, he'd be as thrilled to see her play as she'd be to have him in the audience. And, considering all the money he's spent on her instruments and lessons, he certainly deserves to be there.

"I mean, think how chuffed Tylor will be," says Sorrel, reading her thoughts. "And he is the one who encourages you. He cares about your music. Doesn't he deserve to see he's right? Doesn't he deserve to have people congratulate him on being your dad?"

Celeste makes an oh-come-on face. "And who's going to know he's my dad unless he holds up a sign?"

"Everybody. They'll know because he's the guy jumping to his feet to give you a standing ovation when you finish your solo, that's how they'll know." Sorrel picks up Celeste's phone from the bedside table and hands it to her. "Go on. Call him."

"I don't know." Celeste stares at the phone, which, suddenly, isn't a sophisticated means of communication but the serpent in the Garden of Eden – *Go on, just take one bite.* "I don't think my mom'd be too happy if he says he can come."

"What's the big deal? You're going to see him over Christmas anyway. So he comes before instead of after." Maybe it isn't the phone that's the serpent. "And he'll be happy even if Lilah won't. Anyway, it's a big auditorium. Maybe she won't notice he's there."

"Ha!" Lilah would notice Tylor if he were wearing a disguise and the auditorium were the size of a football stadium. "What if he doesn't answer?"

Sorrel groans. "Then you leave him a message. But hurry, Cel. Ms Santos will be here soon."

Not three minutes after Tylor picks up, Astra and Winnie burst into the bedroom, loaded down with bags, as excited as hunters after a record kill. They dump the bags on Astra's bed, then rush out again because shopping has made them ravenous. Celeste, deep in her conversation with her father, barely notices either their arrival or departure. Tylor, as predicted, is thrilled. Thrilled that he's been invited to the concert. Thrilled that Celeste has a solo and a spot with the blues band.

"We'll video the whole thing," says Celeste's father. "This is going to be a historic occasion. Your first official public appearance."

And Celeste says, "We? You mean you and Jake?"

"Sure thing. He's not going to want to miss this."

"Oh," says Celeste. She doesn't remember Jake being part of the plan.

"Don't worry about your mom," says Tylor. "It's been a long time now, and this is a special occasion. We're coming to your graduation in June, so why shouldn't we come to this?"

"I didn't know that," says Celeste. "About graduation."

Her father laughs. "That's because I just decided. In any case, I'm sure your mom'll be fine with it. Like I said, it's been a long time."

It isn't until she hangs up that Celeste realizes: probably the time hasn't been long enough. Her mother is standing solidly in the doorway.

"Astra said you were on the phone. Who were you talking to?" It sounds like an innocent question, as if she has no idea who was on the other end, but her smile shines like a brand new trap.

"Don't bother lying," advises Sorrel. "She knows."

"Dad," says Celeste.

Lilah continues to smile and sound as if she was born only yesterday – possibly late in the afternoon. "Really? Again? You only just talked to him."

"Yeah. But he forgot to tell me something." Celeste chews on her bottom lip for a second. "He's going to come to the Christmas concert."

"Is he?" If Lilah's smile were a balloon, it would burst. "And is he bringing that man with him?"

"Jake," says Celeste. "His name's Jake. I don't know. I didn't actually invite him."

"You know how hurtful I find this, don't you, darling? How difficult it is having your father in my world like that?" It would be impossible for an independent observer to judge how hurtful or difficult that is, as she keeps right on smiling. "You might at least have asked me first. Considered my feelings."

"Here we go…" says Sorrel.

"I'm sorry. I didn't mean— It was just— I said I had to go to rehearsal soon and he asked for what and I told him all about the concert and then he said he'd love to come, and I just couldn't not invite him, could I? I mean, he was going to visit for Christmas anyway. This is just a little sooner."

"Rehearsal?" repeats Lilah. "You have a rehearsal this evening?"

Celeste nods. "Yeah. I told you. We're having a full rehearsal every weekend till the concert."

"But not tonight," and suddenly her smile is her professional one; *there's no way you're breaking this lease.*

Celeste must know what her mother is saying – she has heard it before – but somehow doesn't understand. "Yes. Ms Santos is coming to get me. I told you."

"Oh, but I need you to stay home tonight."

She has heard this before, too.

"Why? I didn't know."

"I have plans for tonight," says her mother. "I thought I told you." Her sigh is the sigh of a woman who puts up with a lot. "Maybe I forgot. You know how busy I am. I'm only one person. I can't always keep track of everything."

"I'm sorry. But I don't think you did tell me. I really don't remember—"

"Well, I'm sorry if you don't remember, Celeste, but I'm afraid you have to be here," says Lilah. "Winnie's spending the night. You know they're too young to be left by themselves."

"They're not too young, they're just too dangerous," says Sorrel. "She doesn't dare leave them alone."

"But I have to go," says Celeste. "It's important. The concert—"

"Surely you can miss one rehearsal," says Lilah. "It's not like you're going to forget how to play the violin in one week."

"My solo's on the piano," says Celeste.

"You're not going to forget how to play that either. I'll tell you what." Lilah has come up with the perfect solution. "Why don't you order pizza for supper? So you don't have to cook."

"She wasn't going to cook," says Sorrel to the oblivious Lilah. "You were. Celeste was going out."

"It's too bad you haven't made any new friends," says Lilah, "or you could have one of them come over to keep you company." She glances at her watch. "Will you look at the time? I have to get going."

As soon as Lilah leaves the room Sorrel says, "I have another great idea. You want to hear it?"

"Not really." Celeste is newly aware that what she used to think of as resilience in herself is simply resignation.

"Call Ruben."

"Ruben? I don't want company, Sorrel. Besides, I have to call Ms Santos. Tell her I can't make it tonight."

"No, you have to call Ruben. Ask him to come and stand guard over the gruesome twosome till you get back."

"He won't do it. He hasn't been over here in a year. And he hardly ever leaves his house at night. And—"

"Maybe he'll surprise you. It can't hurt to ask."

The contact picture for Ruben, put on before Celeste knew he'd given up on art, is a painting of Venice by John Singer Sargent. Celeste hits Call, and turns her back on Sorrel. "I have a problem," she says when Ruben answers. "I have rehearsal tonight, for the concert, but my mom has to go out and Astra has Winnie staying over. And, you know, they can't really be left alone. I mean, you know what Astra's like. And Winnie's even worse. They do whatever they get in their heads. Even when someone's here they can get out of hand... Yeah, exactly, I forgot about that. Like the time they locked us all out of the house. But that was a while ago. Now they're more likely to lock us in. Anyway, I was wondering if..."

As it happens, Celeste has caught Ruben in one of those moments when every thought seems to have some regret attached to it. Across the hall, his mother's typewriter clatters on, and Ruben's mind rolls on – thinking of his dad, thinking of Sylvia, thinking of his friends. Thinking of Paul Klee working despite the pain; of Van Gogh shooting himself in the chest. Remembering Sorrel saying that he's running away from life. Thinking of ending up with nothing. And then his phone rings, and he looks down to see Celeste smiling back at him. He's not the only one with problems. "So you want me to come over and watch them while you go to rehearsal?" asks Ruben.

Celeste stares at the phone. She definitely wasn't expecting him to volunteer.

"For God's sake," hisses Sorrel. "Say yes!"

"Yes," says Celeste. "That would be great. I know it's short notice and everything. And it's raining. And Astra and Winnie can be a real challenge. And—"

"Consider me on my way," says Ruben.

When Celeste turns back to Sorrel, expecting to see an I-told-you-so look on her face, there is no one there.

Sorrel knows she told her so; she doesn't need to say it again.

24

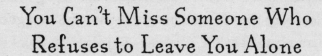

You Can't Miss Someone Who Refuses to Leave You Alone

The Gwinnets' car pulls into the drive; the engine cuts and the headlamps go off. Bernard Gwinnet climbs out of the driver's seat and slams the door so that anyone hearing it will know that he's not in a very good mood. His wife and son get out quickly, and follow him to the house in the silence you'd expect if the world had just ended. This post-apocalyptic absence of sound has been with them since they left the school, and, if experience is anything to go by, could last for several days. Officer Gwinnet is not a particularly generous man, but when he's angry and unhappy he likes to make sure that everyone shares that rage and unhappiness with him.

Tonight was the first game of the season, and the Beacons didn't win. Didn't win in the way that the Axis countries in World War II didn't win. Orlando took as long as he could to shower and change into his street clothes, but his parents didn't give up and leave without him. They were waiting for him in the lobby as always. His mother was smiling hopefully, but without conviction. His father looked like a ticking bomb.

Orlando hurried up to them. "I'm sorry, Dad. I guess we had a bad night."

Which was when his father spoke for the last time. "Is that what you think?" He spat the words from his mouth as if they were a bad piece of meat. "What I think is that you're a disgrace to the memory of your brother. What I think is that God took the wrong son."

Suzanne nervously patted his arm, as if he was the one who needed comforting, but he shook her off and strode out to the car, just as he shakes her off now when she offers him a nice hot drink, and marches upstairs, an unforgiving storm of a man still in his parka and baseball cap.

"He didn't mean what he said," Orlando's mother whispers as they watch Bernard disappear around the landing. "He's just upset."

Of course he meant it. Orlando has always known that if his father had been asked which son he wanted taken from him he wouldn't have chosen Raylan, but it's never been said out loud before. Which makes a difference. Just as the parents of a missing child will never give up hope until they see the body, until his father said those words it was possible to pretend he never thought them.

"I know. It's okay." Orlando kisses his mother's cheek. "I'm wiped out, Mom. I'm going to bed."

But, as always, his mother hasn't stopped trying to make things better. "And he knows you're not to blame for losing the game. He knows that. He just cares so much."

Cares so much about the game.

"Yeah, I know." Of course it's Orlando's fault. The Beacons didn't just lose against their arch-rivals, the Willes Wildcats, the county champs; they were decimated, humiliated and generally made to look as if a Brownie troop could have done better. Basketball may be a team sport, but Orlando is the Beacons' star player, and the only way he could have played worse was if he'd actually managed to score points for the other side. The rest of the Beacons played badly, too, but he can't help feeling that they were following his lead – a lead that led straight to defeat.

It's either ironic or a further example of how unfair life can be that this has happened despite the fact that ever since that first practice, Orlando has been working harder than ever. Determined. Focused. Single-minded. Disciplined. He's managed a few dance practices and one meeting of the Peakston Players, but, that aside, has kept his mind and his energy on honing his skills getting that ball through that hoop, and making sure the other team doesn't. And it worked. In practice games he's never played better. Never played better, and has refused to think about Sorrel even for a second. Which has also worked. She's stayed away. And she stayed away tonight. His fear that he would be out on the court and suddenly look over to see her sitting in the bleachers, cheering him on, was totally unfounded. No, in a further example of irony pushed to its limits, it wasn't the sight of Sorrel smiling at him that ruined his game. It was the sight of his father – leaning forward, clenched and white with tension, looking as if the future of mankind depended on what happened that night in the Beaconspoint High School gym. Orlando didn't just lose the will to win, he lost the will to play. He saw the intense expressions on the faces of the other players and the intense expressions on the faces of the spectators and the take-no-prisoners expression on the face of his father, and all he could think was: *What am I doing here?*

Orlando slowly climbs the stairs, wanting nothing more than to pull the covers over his head and forget for a while that this night ever happened. But, of course, it isn't over yet. He opens the door to his bedroom, and there is Sorrel, stretched out on his bed, wearing jeans and a Beaconsfield High sweatshirt, watching a film on his laptop.

"I take it you guys lost," says Sorrel, hitting Pause.

Has the news of his defeat spread even to the spirit world? "What makes you say that?"

She looks amused; which makes one of them. "I have telepathic powers. And besides that, the temperature dropped like a hundred degrees when Officer Gwinnet came upstairs. So I'm guessing he's blaming you."

Orlando kicks off his shoes and sits down in the chair at his desk. "Well maybe he's right."

"How's that? You mean you were the only player on the team?"

"I mean maybe I should've been an inspiration and not a drag on them. Maybe I should've worked harder." Instead of giving ninety-eight per cent, give a hundred and fifty per cent.

Sorrel sits up. "Or maybe your dad should've been some big sports hero himself instead of making his kids do it for him. Like my mom should've been a supermodel instead of getting knocked up with the twins and getting married."

"Go away, Sorrel. I have enough on my mind right now. I don't need you needling me."

"I'm not needling you. I'm trying to make you stop feeling like everything's your fault. So you had a bad game. So what?"

"So I shouldn't've."

"Shouldn't, couldn't, wouldn't..." She shakes her head back and forth. "You know what the Taoists say, don't you?"

The Taoists? Suddenly she's quoting Taoist philosophy at him?

"I'm guessing it has nothing to do with basketball."

She sticks her tongue out at him. "In basketball as in life, Orlando." And then she just sits there, her head tilting to one side, staring at him with eyes that never blink.

"Okay, I give up. What do the Taoists say?"

"The Taoists say that shit happens."

"Well, there's a revelation. How many centuries did it take them to work that one out?"

"You're missing the point as usual," says Sorrel. "Shit happens. Things you can't do anything about. Things that are out of your control."

"Now you're missing the point! How can you not see that? This was in my control."

"I didn't mean the game. I meant your brother."

"For the love of God, will you go away?" He seems to have moved from depression to anger. "Just go away and leave me alone!"

The only answer is a very gentle knock on his door.

"Orlando?" His mother is whispering. "Orlando, are you all right, honey?"

He takes three deep breaths, gets up and opens the door so she can see that he's all right. "I'm fine, Mom." He's whispering, too, now. "I was just, you know, talking to myself. You go back to bed."

When he turns to the room, Sorrel, of course, is gone.

Proving that she can do as she's told. When she wants to.

25

It's Beginning to Look
a Lot like Christmas

~

December

After Sorrel reminded him about it, Ruben found himself constantly thinking about the painting he did of the four of them trying to get the Gwinnets' neighbour's cat out of that tree. What did he do with it? Where could it be? He's looked everywhere possible, to the point where Sylvia was standing in the hallway outside his bedroom door wanting to know what he was doing, he was making such a racket – but, unlike Sorrel, it had disappeared without a trace.

It's only today, when he gets home from school, that Ruben remembers the closet at the top of the stairs. It's where Sylvia keeps all the copies of her books – author's copies, reprints, foreign editions – and he certainly has no memory of putting it in there, but that, of course, doesn't mean that he didn't. So, after he checks on his mother and grabs something to eat, he takes a torch and starts his search. He's standing on a box of books, reaching for a stack of folders on the top shelf, when he loses his balance, drops the torch and stumbles to the floor. Disoriented and unable to tell where the floor ends and the staircase begins, he steps onto air and tumbles down the stairs, ending in a heap at the bottom.

Ruben sits up – gingerly – not sure whether or not he is hurt or merely surprised.

"What happened?" His mother is on the landing, lantern held high, peering down through the shadows. "Are you all right, honey?"

"I'm fine, Mom. I just kind of fell." He rolls his shoulders, moves his hands, winces when he flexes his left foot.

"You fell standing on the floor?"

"Actually," says Ruben, "I was standing on—"

"You know, I'm a little worried about you." She's worried about *him*? "Always talking to yourself... Thumping around... Losing your balance like that... Are you having headaches? Dizzy spells?"

"No, Mom, I was—"

He breaks off from his second attempt to explain that he was standing on a box because, for the first time in nearly a year, Gaia Pendragon leaves the safety of the enchanted tower that is the second floor and comes down as far as the bottom of the stairs. Being Sylvia Rossi; being mom. Feeling his ankles. She looks around bewilderedly, as if only just noticing how dark it is. "There's not much light here, is there?" Not much, as in none. "You could've broken your neck falling like that." She carefully helps him stand, making him lean on her. "What on earth were you doing? Were you looking for something in the closet?"

He and Sylvia don't talk about the past. The past is always with them, of course – a herd of elephants crowded into their little house, crapping all over and almost heroically ignored – but there's no *Remember that time... Remember when Dad...* As if touching the wound will make it bleed.

But it's so unusual for her to be looking after him – for her to be worried about him – that when she asks what he was doing he tells her the truth. Searching for the past.

To his surprise, rather than recoil in horror, she smiles. "Of course I know where that painting is. It's in my office."

Ruben hobbles back upstairs to her room with her, bruised but definitely not broken. She swings the lantern towards the far wall. "It's right there."

Ruben looks where she's pointing, and there it is, right there in plain sight, but disguised by the general gloom as just another picture handed down through the family with nowhere else to go – like the paint-by-numbers boat at sunset he did when he was three and the cover of his mother's first published novel. Right there all the time, the one place he never thought of looking. Orlando, Sorrel, Celeste and him, caught for ever as they were right then – never to change, never to disappear, never to grow old and never to die. But the image is more than just a copy of that moment. Ruben isn't a camera, freezing time. His painting has added something to the photograph. It's added him, how he saw them all, how he felt about them, how they actually were.

"I love that painting. It always cheers me up." The lantern light falls on the four friends, the cat and the tree. "Look how happy you all are."

"Yeah," he agrees. "We were all pretty happy."

She doesn't turn to him, but says, "Don't you miss them, Ruben? They never come over any more. Not even Orlando."

"I see them at school. Well, you know, not Sorrel…" Which is truer than his mother can possibly imagine. "But everybody else. So, no, I don't miss them. I see them all the time."

"I miss them," says Sylvia. "They were always laughing and fooling around. Full of life."

"Yeah, well, you know… It's a busy year."

And then, still gazing at that moment – Orlando telling Ruby not to worry; Ruben telling Orlando to for

God's sake hurry up before he drops him; Sorrel and Celeste laughing too much to speak – Sylvia says, "Are you going to paint another picture this year?"

Ruben continues looking at the picture on the wall, but suddenly his mind's eye is seeing the photo of them all at Sorrel's birthday party, long ago last June.

"You mean for Christmas?" Not only has he given less than no thought to doing another painting, it never occurred to him they'd be celebrating Christmas. In the dark? "Are we doing Christmas this year?"

"Of course we are." She sounds as if he's the one who's consistently unreasonable and out of touch with reality. She turns from the painting to the painter. "When did we decide not to celebrate Christmas this year?"

When you took all the light bulbs out of their sockets and cancelled it last year.

"I hadn't thought about another painting." Why would he? He was under the impression that they'd given up Christmas as totally as he's given up art. Although perhaps he hasn't given it up that totally; it isn't true that he threw everything out. He'd sooner cut off his ear. His paints and crayons, chalks and brushes are all in the attic. "Maybe," says Ruben. "Maybe I'll do another one."

For most people, the word "maybe" means possibly. Perhaps. It could happen, but, then again, it might not.

I'll think about it and see what I decide. Watch this space. Sorrel Groober used to be one of those people, but now, of course, she isn't. Ruben wasn't aware of her presence when he and Sylvia were looking at his painting, but she must have been lurking in the shadows because when he gets to his room, there she is, going through the photos he's put on his computer.

"Your mother's a genius," she says, knowing he's there without having to bother looking around. "This is such a great idea. Look, here are the pictures from the party. One of them would be perfect. I mean, it's sad, too, of course. You know, my last birthday and everything, but that day wasn't sad. That day was awesome."

She's worn him down so much by now that Ruben doesn't even think of telling her to get off his computer, or to go away, or to for-the-love-of-God leave him alone. He doesn't even ask how she knows what he was thinking. He says, "I didn't say I was going to do it. I said I'd think about it."

"And disappoint your mom? Now? When she's starting to loosen up? Are you crazy?"

Yes, he may very well be crazy, but that's turning out to be the least of his problems.

"Loosen up?" His efforts to control his life – to be completely responsible, to make safe, sure choices, to live by plan not whim or intuition – seem to be going the way of the dodo and the dinosaur. "What are you talking about – loosen up?"

"You heard her." Sorrel clicks the mouse, and the printer hums. "She noticed how dark it is. You can start putting lights on now, she's not going to freak out."

"Oh, I don't know—"

"Yes you do." As the pictures she's chosen begin to print, Sorrel looks around at him. "She's worried about you. Don't you get it? She's worried about *you*, not about herself." Sorrel grins. "Because you're talking to yourself and being weird falling down the stairs and stuff! How fantastic is that?"

"I've been trying not to worry her. I—"

"And that's worked just brilliantly, hasn't it?" Her voice and expression are in perfect harmony: withering contempt. "That's really ripped the space blankets off the windows. Instead of involving her you've let her slip away." She stands up. "Come on, you have to get your painting gear so you can get started."

"I thought I told you. I got rid of it all."

"No you didn't. You're not that big a jerk."

"How can you be sure?"

"I'm waiting, Ruben." Because she's folded her arms in front of her she looks as if she's tapping her foot.

Impatiently. "So where'd you stash it? Basement? Attic? Garage?"

You can fight City Hall. You can fight a parking ticket. You can fight an unfair grade. But you can't fight someone who isn't there.

"Attic."

"Bring a bulb for the landing light," Sorrel orders. "We don't want you falling down the stairs again."

The two of them are in the attic, searching among the boxes for the one that holds all his tools and materials when he hears his mother in the hallway below, calling his name.

"Ruben? Ruben, honey? Are you up there?"

He gives Sorrel a now-you've-done-it look. He knew it. Why does he listen to someone who got herself run over? His mother's upset that the light is on in the hall.

"Yeah, Mom." He goes to the opening and looks down, Sorrel beside him, looking down, too. His mother's at the bottom of the folding ladder, her trusty lantern hanging unneeded from her hand. "I thought I might do that picture like you suggested. I stored all my art stuff up here."

"Oh, that's what you're doing." She nods. "I wasn't sure. But I was thinking, while you're there, maybe you could find those lights your dad used to put up every

Christmas. The red and green ones? I'm pretty sure they're up there somewhere."

"I'll have a look," says Ruben.

When he turns back to Sorrel she couldn't look more supercilious if she were a Divine Right King. "I should've bet you she wouldn't be freaked. Maybe from now on you'll actually listen to me."

"I wouldn't count on it," says Ruben.

26

The Truth at Last

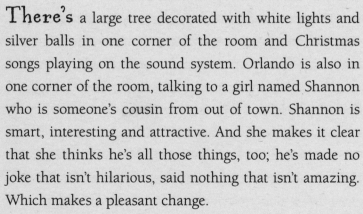

There's a large tree decorated with white lights and silver balls in one corner of the room and Christmas songs playing on the sound system. Orlando is also in one corner of the room, talking to a girl named Shannon who is someone's cousin from out of town. Shannon is smart, interesting and attractive. And she makes it clear that she thinks he's all those things, too; he's made no joke that isn't hilarious, said nothing that isn't amazing. Which makes a pleasant change.

It's two weeks before Christmas, and this is Coach Mena's annual party for the basketball squad. Orlando is here because he had to come (there would have been two more weeks of silence from his father if he didn't show some team spirit), and because he thought the party would cheer him up. This isn't the unhappiest day in an unhappy year, but it is definitely in the line-up. Exactly twelve months ago, while he was driving himself crazy trying to find the perfect gift for her, Sorrel broke up with him. They'd had three amazing weeks together when, his hormones having the time of their lives, he'd never felt better – like he was the coolest, greatest, nicest, best-looking guy who had ever lived – and then, without so much as a ten-minute warning, it was all over. Just like that. Here today and gone tomorrow. Big winner one minute; loser the next. ☹ was all she wrote.

The party hasn't stopped him from remembering what day this is, but it is making him feel slightly less bad about it. Shannon's attention, although largely unwanted, is nonetheless appreciated. He's not a complete waste of space; some girls like him.

But somewhere around the fifth time Bing Crosby sings "White Christmas", Orlando has an overwhelming desire to be home. "You know," he says, as Bing wishes once again that they have snow on the twenty-fifth, "I think I'm going to get going. I feel like I'm getting a headache. There's so much noise."

"That's perfect. I'm pretty done here, too. I'll get my coat." She has a really nice smile. "You can walk me home."

This was so not in his plans that he misunderstands her. "I thought you live in Chester."

Her look says he's hopeless, but endearing. "Not

tonight, I don't." She gives him an affectionate punch in the arm. "Tonight I live a few blocks away. Remember? I'm Selby Rider's cousin?"

"Oh, yeah. Of course."

It's a cold, star-bright night. Shannon puts her arm through his, and they walk slowly, looking at the decorations on the houses – Santa and his elves on porches and in windows, reindeer on the rooftops, a bedazzle of lights across windows and lawns – Shannon doing a good job of holding up both sides of the conversation. When they get to the Riders' she says, "I'm here all weekend. If you want to do something." She's standing so close he can make a pretty good guess at what she's been eating. "Maybe you could show me the town."

"Yeah, I – I could do that." She's nice, she's pretty, she likes him, he likes her – and she is very definitely waiting to be kissed. What could make him feel better than that? He leans towards her.

And there, standing in the driveway smiling at them, is Sorrel, all dressed up for a winter night in a plaid jacket and matching hat. He jumps back so fast he hits the giant illuminated candy cane behind him.

"What's wrong? Are you okay?"

"Yeah, I'm fine. It's nothing I—" It's just that I can't kiss you with my dead girlfriend watching. "My head."

And now it really is starting to throb. "I really have to go."

"But—"

"I have your number, Shannon. I'll ring you. I'll show you the town."

And he is off the stoop and on the front path as fast as possible without running. He turns when he reaches the pavement. Shannon is standing staring after him. He waves. "I'll give you a call!"

"So she seems nice." Sorrel is right beside him as he starts down the street.

"You have to ruin everything, don't you?" His breath makes tiny clouds in front of them. "Why can't you just leave me alone? Why can't you stay wherever it is you are when you aren't hassling me?"

"Me? What'd I do?"

"You know damn well what you did. Nobody invited you to the party."

"I wasn't at the party. That's not really my scene any more."

"Oh, excuse me. You weren't at the party. But you're here now. So I guess your new scene is interfering in my life."

"You didn't really want to kiss her. It was pretty obvious. Not to her, maybe, but to a casual observer." Sorrel skips a few steps to keep up with him. "So, really, you should be thanking me. I did you a favour."

He refuses to look at her. "You never do me any favours. All you do is mess everything up."

Suddenly she's in front of him, walking backwards. "Oh, I get it. You're still sore at me, aren't you? Because I dumped you. That's why you're mad at me. Not because I interrupted your big kiss."

"Don't be so full of yourself. That isn't why I'm pissed off. I'm pissed off because for some reason now that you're dead you won't stop bothering me."

"I knew it. I always knew it. You never really got over me. You always thought we'd get back together, didn't you?"

"No, of course not." He didn't think, he hoped. "But it would've been nice if you'd told me why we broke up. If you'd had the decency to let me in on the story instead of acting like I wasn't involved."

"I did tell you."

"No you didn't. You said it wasn't me, it was you. Which is like the oldest phoney line in the book. Everybody says that so they spare your feelings and don't have to get into a big argument."

"Except that it wasn't a phoney line." She's wearing her favourite dangling gold star earrings. They sway when she moves, flashing in the street lamps. "It was true. It was me. It was totally me."

On the day before Sorrel sent him the break-up text they'd gone back to her house after school. Since they'd started dating the only times he'd been in her house (briefly) were when he was picking her up to go somewhere. Which hadn't bothered him as much as it might have. They all avoided going to Sorrel's house whenever possible because her mother was almost always there – and there was almost always a scene. How long it took for Sorrel and her mother to start fighting depended on everybody's mood or whether Meryl had had an early cocktail or not, but it rarely took long enough to finish a soda. He went with her on that afternoon because Sorrel wanted his opinion on the project she was doing for art. And, like a gift from the gods, that day they had the place to themselves. He wouldn't have to leave because he was embarrassed or because Sorrel was too angry to want him around. They went up to her room – the first and last time he would ever be in it. She got out her project and they talked about it for a while, and then they started making out. Which also wasn't something that happened a lot. Thinking about it later, he reckoned that he got a little carried away, but at the time he thought she pushed him off her because she heard her mother come home. She was up first, pulling her clothes together. Saying they'd better go down. He was surprised to discover that her mother hadn't come home, but before he could suggest going back to her room and finishing what they'd started she said he'd better leave. She kissed him goodbye, but not the way she'd been kissing him ten minutes before. Or maybe it was not the way that he'd been kissing her. And at 1.45 a.m. she sent him a text: *I think we should stop dating. I'm really sorry. It's nothing to do with you. It's me. We're better off friends* ☹. Merry Christmas.

Now he says, "Well that's not what it felt like to me." Especially when he practically begged her to give him another chance and she refused. "It felt like it was my fault."

"Because you weren't paying attention. You were only thinking about how you felt; you never thought about me," says Sorrel. "I always really liked you, Orlando. You know that. I liked you a lot. I still do. I just never liked you that way. You're a great guy. But not for me. I was into somebody else."

Knowing that he's a great guy for someone else doesn't keep the bitterness out of his voice. "Then why did you go out with me if you never liked me that way? Why lead me on?"

"I didn't mean to. But I had to go out with somebody. You can't be the girl all the guys want to date and not go out with somebody. Everybody expected it. Especially my mom. She never got off my case. And my mom wanted me to date you." Despite the fights, Sorrel did what her mother told her to do – just as Orlando does what Officer Gwinnet wants. "Meryl was always on at me about you. *Orlando this… Orlando that…* Maybe she really does like you." Her laugh sputters. "She probably likes you more than she ever liked me. You know, because you're good-looking and a sports star. She figured we were a perfect match. Beauty and the Jock." They've both stopped walking and are stood facing each other. "And if it worked out, and you became a big basketball legend and I was this mega model, then it was win–win all the way, wasn't it?"

That depended on how you looked at it. One person's win–win could be another's lose–lose.

"But what about me? What about my feelings? Did you ever consider how I felt?"

"Of course I did. That's why I ended it. I could see you were starting to get serious. I was trying to save you from being hurt."

And look how well that turned out.

"If you're trying to make me feel better it isn't working."

But maybe it is. Because suddenly he sees very clearly that the enthusiasm was all on his side. In that short time when they dated Sorrel had treated him exactly as she'd always treated him – like a buddy, like a good and close friend. The only difference was that sometimes she'd link her arm with his when they were walking together, or even hold his hand. And she'd let him kiss her – only now he isn't sure if she really kissed him back. Because he finally gets it, sees the pattern. All the guys Sorrel went out with – never for more than a few weeks, if that long – all big men at school; guys her mother would approve of, probably guys her mother picked the same way she picked him. Somewhere way at the back of his mind, images are stirring. Sorrel really happy. Sorrel really excited. Sorrel really involved. Sorrel smiling like she knew the best secret there ever was.

"So who was it you really wanted to go out with?" asks Orlando. "Who was it you liked that way?"

She tilts her head to one side. "Can't you guess?"

On either side of them the coloured lights glow and the bare, iced branches of the trees shine. In front of him, Sorrel gazes back at him calmly, the gold stars glinting against the darkness. Of course. The earrings. A gift from Celeste. And he sees the two of them at the birthday party, heads together; hears Sorrel say she's eighteen and can do what she wants. How could he have missed it? Celeste and Sorrel; Sorrel and Celeste. Inseparable; close as the bricks in a wall. A match guaranteed to displease both their mothers.

"Celeste," says Orlando. It was always Celeste. It really wasn't about him.

"I knew you'd be able to guess," says Sorrel.

A door shuts on Orlando's right, and he turns to see two French bull terriers and a man in a green parka on the porch decorated with glowing snowmen. The dogs hurl themselves down the steps, pulling the man behind them. As they pass, the man gives Orlando the wary sort of smile you'd give someone who's been standing for some time on an empty street talking earnestly to himself as they pass.

27

The Peace on Earth Blues

Celeste is nervous and excited. After months of preparation, the night of the Christmas concert has arrived. Everyone involved in the concert has worked and practised hard for it, but none harder than Celeste. She wants to make her father proud, but she also wants to make her mother proud. To show Lilah that music isn't just a hobby for her; that it's what she's good at; that it's what she wants to do. This concert means so much to Celeste that she's been able to think of nothing else all day. Her mother and sister talk to her, but she has no idea what they're saying. She goes into a room, and then has no idea why she's there. She is so distracted that she could have had a complete makeover in the time it's taken her to get ready.

Now, however, Celeste, Sorrel and Celeste's guitar are in the living room. The guitar is wearing an angel sticker on its case. Celeste is wearing a long, flowing, red tunic over a long, flowing, red skirt and earrings like the ones she gave Sorrel last year, but in silver not gold. Sorrel is wearing a reindeer onesie – something she always wanted that her mother wouldn't let her have. This time Celeste knows exactly why she is here. She and her guitar are waiting for Ruben to pick them up. After categorically saying that he was no longer interested in working on school productions, Ruben suddenly changed his mind and agreed to design the sets for the concert. The musicians have to get to the school early to get ready, and because he wants to check everything one last time Ruben offered to give her a lift. Sorrel stands at the window, acting as lookout. They both turn as Celeste's mother comes in, glancing at her watch.

Time is a peculiar thing. More a fluid than a solid, minutes can seem like hours, and hours can seem like the blink of an eye. Which is a roundabout way of saying that though Tylor Redwing may think that he and Lilah have been apart long enough for the debris of their break-up to have passed under the bridge and crossed several seas by now, that is not how Lilah sees it. She has accepted the fact that he is making his Christmas visit early so that he can attend Celeste's concert – and that she will have to be in the same room with him in front of her friends and clients – but acceptance isn't the same as being happy about it. Her only official statement has been, "It's a free country. I can't stop him from coming." But she would if she could, and both she and Celeste know that. Which is why she hasn't been told that Jake is coming, too.

"What time did Ruben—" Lilah is saying, but breaks off when she sees Celeste. She tilts her head at an angle of disapproval. "You don't think that outfit is a little informal for a concert?" Her smile is helpful. "I thought orchestras always wore black and white."

"She's thinking of penguins," says Sorrel. "The Philharmonic Penguin Orchestra."

Celeste smiles back. "No, I don't think it's too informal. I think it's perfect." Sorrel helped her pick it out. Casual, but not too casual; colourful enough for a blues band, but not too colourful for a serious solo. "I told you, it's all about the music. And Ms Santos doesn't believe in following outmoded conventions."

"Um." Thinking of her ex-husband brings to mind several outmoded conventions that Lilah believes in following.

"Christmas is a celebration," says Celeste. "Ms Santos said we should look like we're at a party, not a funeral."

"Well, I hope you do have something to celebrate. I hope your father's not too late. You know how unreliable he is."

"He's not going to be late. He had a flat tyre, that's all. I told you, he fixed it right away."

Lilah frowns. "I don't remember him being that handy before. He could barely change a light bulb when he lived with us. Do you remember the time he flooded the bathroom trying to stop the tap from dripping? And the ti—"

"Ruben's here," announces Sorrel. "And not a second too soon."

Celeste picks up her coat from the arm of the sofa. "I'll see you later, Mom. I have to go." She gives Lilah a quick kiss as Ruben sounds his horn. "Don't forget, it starts at seven sharp."

Sorrel's antlers wave as she turns away from the window. "You may be sorry you reminded her," says Sorrel.

The auditorium is almost full and the lights slightly dimmed as the orchestra takes its seats onstage for the first half of the programme. Celeste scans the crowd for familiar faces. Her mother and Astra sit in the middle with Lilah's friends from work. Orlando and Suzanne Gwinnet sit with Ruben on the opposite side of the aisle. Lilah keeps glancing over her shoulder, which means that the reason Celeste doesn't spot her father is because he isn't there. She'll never hear the end of it if her mother is right and Tylor doesn't make the concert after all. But then, as Ms Santos takes the stage, the doors open at the back and Tylor and Jake appear, framed for a second in the doorway, looking out of place in their jeans, leather jackets and Christmas ties among the suit jackets and slacks of the other men in the audience. It isn't just Celeste's mother who looks over as they stride down the aisle to the miraculously (or, possibly, unfortunately) empty seats at the front. But it is Lilah who gets Celeste's attention; her expression the mix of horror and surprise you would experience if, in the middle of a torturous nightmare, you suddenly realized that you aren't asleep. Celeste really should have told her Jake was coming. Ms Santos raises her baton. Sparing Celeste from seeing the look her mother shoots her way.

It may or may not be true, as the playwright William Congreve said, that music has charms to soothe the savage breast, but it definitely has enough charm to make Celeste forget about anything else. And from the reception both parts of the programme receive, it seems that music's charms work on the audience as well. At the very end, when all the musicians come out onstage, they are given a standing ovation. The first people on their feet are Tylor and Jake; the first and the loudest.

Celeste has done such a good job of forgetting

anything but the concert that it isn't until she and her guitar emerge to find her family in the foyer that the happiness of tonight's success walks straight into a wall. Here, clearly, is something she should have thought of before. The two sides stand facing each other like duellists. Her father seems to be doing most of the talking, Jake smiling and nodding beside him. Lilah also is smiling, but like a woman carved out of stone; Astra is by the doors, talking to some kids she knows from school.

"There she is!" Tylor wraps her – and the guitar – in a hug. "You were great, honey. Absolutely fantastic."

Jake holds up his video camera. "And we have the whole thing recorded here for posterity." And then he takes his turn at hugging.

Lilah smiles at Celeste. "I'm sure you must be ex—."

Tylor cuts her off. "I was just saying to your mom that we should all go out and celebrate." He moves his hand between him and Jake. "Our treat. Just name the place."

"And I was just saying to your father that we've already eaten—"

Celeste was too wound up to eat supper. "I haven't—"

"But you're tired," says Lilah. "You've been working so much for tonight. All those rehearsals. All that practice. I'm sure you'd like to get an early night."

"We don't have to stay out late," says Tylor. "We can

just go get a pizza. Give us all a chance to catch up."

Lilah looks as though she'd rather catch the plague. "I'm afraid you'll have to count me and Astra out. We really aren't hungry." She turns her Mount Rushmore smile on her daughter. "But if Celeste wants to go that's up to her, of course."

Three pairs of eyes focus on Celeste. She would love to go out with her father and Jake. She would also love not to have her mother looking at her like that, as if Celeste is twisting a knife in her back. Celeste can feel guilt sucking all the joy of the last two hours from her heart.

"Of course," Lilah says to Tylor, still smiling at Celeste, "you are going to see them both tomorrow. You could celebrate then." If anyone's twisting a knife in anyone's back it isn't Celeste.

Celeste looks from the men to her mother. She can't leave Lilah to drive home alone. And she will see her father and Jake tomorrow. And she is pretty tired; it's been a long day.

She opens her mouth to say that she thinks she'd better go home, but the voice she hears is Sorrel's.

"Are you kidding me?" Still in her onesie, Sorrel is standing just behind Lilah. "Your dad and Jake came all this way to see you play, and you're going to go home because your mom wants to punish you and them? You should go celebrate. Believe me, you'll have plenty of time to feel guilty tomorrow." Sorrel's antlers bob. "Didn't I tell you you'd regret reminding your mom to be on time?"

Celeste leans over and gives her mother a kiss. "I'll see you later," she says. "You don't have to wait up, I have my keys."

28

Starry, Starry Night

~

January

Sylvia frowns at the screen. Since a few not-too-bright lights have been allowed back on in the house she's started leaving her room more. She won't go into the kitchen yet, but she comes downstairs and eats supper with Ruben in the dining room. Some nights she'll even give him a game of Scrabble or cards, and twice has watched a film with him on his laptop. At Christmas she let him drive her around the neighbourhood to look at all the decorations, talking about all the times the three of them had gone from street to street, always picking up a take-out on the way home. "Remember how much your father loved it?" she asked. Sorrel, in the back seat, said, "I told you so."

Besides this new willingness to see where she's going and to go there, Sylvia has started answering her own emails. The email she's frowning at right now is from the manager of the bookshop in the local mall, telling her how excited they are about her forthcoming author event and including photos of the poster and window display they've made. "I don't remember saying I'd do it," says Sylvia. "Why would I say that? I haven't done anything like that in months. And it's miles away." She looks up at Ruben, who is peering over her shoulder. "Do you remember me saying yes? Do you even remember them asking?"

"I'm not sure. Maybe I was out of that loop. But we can check your old messages, see if they did ask, and if you did reply." He leans across her to move the cursor. And there it is, three emails. The first the shop's request, the third the shop's acknowledgment of her reply, and the second Sylvia's reply: *Thank you so much for your kind invitation. I'd be delighted to do a book signing at your store...* Signed by Gaia Pendragon. "There you go," says Ruben. "It looks like you did agree."

"I still don't remember." She shakes her head. "This is why you have to be careful with electrical things. You can't trust them. Your computer must've answered the invitation itself."

This is true and not true at the same time. It's true in the sense that Ruben's laptop sent the acceptance without any help from Sylvia. But it isn't true that it decided to cut out the middleperson and answer the bookshop itself. It was Ruben who typed out the message and hit Send. A deed that he blames on Sorrel. His mother hadn't been online for a couple of days and he was looking through her mail, just checking. There was more than one request for an author visit. Usually, he automatically deletes them, but Sorrel was right beside him, hassling him as usual. Yapping on and on about how Sylvia was doing a disservice to herself and her fans. How much the Pendragon books mean to her readers. How much better it would make Sylvia feel to realize that. How it would boost her confidence to accept one or two of the invitations she's always receiving. How it would ground her to take on some responsibility. How she might have fun getting out of the house and talking to people again. It would do her several worlds of good. Wasn't it time she faced her fears instead of hiding from them? Wasn't it time she got her life back? And then Sorrel gave him one of her sour, meaningful looks, so he'd know she was talking about more than one life. Which was an example of Sorrel ignoring his efforts to get his own life back, bit by bit. Didn't he leave his mother alone to go keep an eye on Astra and Winnie? Didn't he do the sets for the concert? Didn't he make another painting as his Christmas present for Orlando, Celeste and his mom this year? Hasn't he been making an effort to hang out with Orlando and Celeste? "There's still more to do," said Sorrel. "Maybe a journey starts with the first steps, but it doesn't end with them." He begged her to stop nagging him. "I'll stop if you just say yes to your mom doing one signing," said Sorrel. "The nearest one. That one in the mall. I mean, my God, it's almost the new year. Time for a change." He accepted the invitation as Gaia Pendragon to keep Sorrel quiet, thinking that his mother could always change her mind. Though how he thought she would do that when he never told her about it is another of life's unanswered questions. And then he forgot all about it himself.

"I don't know if I'm up to this," says Sylvia. "It's been so long… Maybe if it was where you work – that nice man—"

"Mr Goldblatt knows them," Ruben lies reassuringly. "He likes them a lot. He says they're really good people."

"I'm sure they are…" She wouldn't care if they were saints. "Maybe if I write back that I have the flu…"

"It's kind of short notice," says Ruben. "The event's only a few days away. They've done all this promotion. Posters. Fliers. Twitter. Facebook. And, like she says in the email, people are really excited. You don't want to disappoint your fans, do you? They'll be really looking forward to meeting you." He squeezes her shoulder. "I'll be with you. You'll be fine."

The cloud of worry lifts a little. "Do you really think so?"

"I know so."

And, for some reason, she believes him.

But come the day and Sylvia isn't fine.

She arrives at breakfast looking as worried as Kandinsky must have when the Nazis started confiscating his paintings, and is too anxious to eat. "I think I really may be getting sick," she tells him. "Maybe I should email them after all. What if I'm contagious? I wouldn't want to infect everybody."

"It's just nerves," says Ruben. "Like you said, it's been a long time. But if you want to call them and cancel... you can't do it by email. Not when they're expecting you in a few hours. That wouldn't be fair."

"Oh." Sylvia stares into her cup. She wasn't counting on actually having to talk to someone. "Maybe you're right. Maybe it's just nerves. I think I'll have another tea."

She spends the rest of the morning getting ready – changing her mind about what she's wearing, not being able to decide on a pair of shoes, misplacing her good-luck necklace – a silver dragon with moonstone eyes – without which she can't possibly leave the house. When at last she's dressed and shod and the dragon is safely around her neck, she's so on edge that it takes twenty minutes to get her into the car because she has to keep going back to make sure the doors are locked, the lights off, the windows shut. He has all he can do to convince her not to have him unplug the fridge since she is suddenly sure that it will explode if there's no one in the house with it.

Ruben slides into the driver's seat and looks over at his mother, paler even than a woman who hasn't been out in daylight for months should be. Why is he making her do this? He should let her go back inside, lock herself in her room, wrap her head in foil. But he doesn't. Is he being selfish? Is it because he likes having meals with her again? Likes being able to leave her when he wants without being doubled over with guilt? Likes seeing her leave her room? Enjoys her company? Doesn't want her to spend the rest of her life upstairs? He makes sure her seat belt's buckled, and drives her to the mall, talking the whole time – babbling really – while she looks out of the window as though she comes from a distant galaxy and this is her first visit to his planet and is taking everything in – and not listening at all. There are a few minutes after he parks when he thinks he may have to drag her from the car, but eventually she gets out, hood up and sunglasses on, holding on to him as if she's afraid of blowing away.

When they reach the shop, there's a queue that stretches from the entrance to the entrance of the next store.

"So many people," whispers Sylvia, cutting off the circulation in his arm. "I didn't think there'd be so many people."

"They're your readers," says Ruben. "They're excited to meet you." And he gently pulls her through the door.

Once inside, she lets the blood flow again. He told them she likes to create an atmosphere in keeping with her books and asked them to keep the lighting low, but they've gone one better and put artificial flickering candles all around the room. "Oh," says Sylvia. "Isn't this pretty? What a nice touch." The staff greets her with enthusiasm and genuine warmth. "I guess Mr Goldblatt was right," says Sylvia.

Ruben learns two important lessons on this momentous afternoon. The first is that his mother is actually very sane. He forgot how intelligent she is – personable and funny, smart and diplomatic, able to handle an onslaught of strangers with good humour and grace (and without once suggesting that someone cover the windows) – because he was so obsessed by her fears. He should have got her help; he should have talked to someone; perhaps he should have talked to her.

The second thing he learns is that a lot of very attractive young women read his mother's books – and that he might like to date some of them – interesting girls, clever girls, pretty girls – but because he was so obsessed with Sorrel he never noticed anyone else.

It's dark by the time they leave the mall. Sylvia walks beside him, no longer gripping his arm as if he's a life preserver, chatting away. "That wasn't so bad," she says as they get in the car. "Everyone was so nice."

And Ruben agrees, "No, it wasn't so bad. And you were brilliant."

They're passing the old country road, once an Indian trail that acted as the highway up here before the real highway was built, when his mother suddenly says, "Ruben, let's go down there. We haven't been on that road in ages. And it's such a nice night."

He doesn't ask why; he knows why. When his dad was alive it was the route he always took when they went for one of their Sunday drives.

She tells him to pull over when they reach the lake his father said was once the site of an Algonquin village. "We used to have picnics here, remember?" says Sylvia. And gets out of the car without being asked.

It is a nice night, cold and clear, the sky aglitter with stars. Ruben puts his arm around his mother and they stand together, looking up at the spangled, timeless heavens – as the trees whisper and the planet turns and the world dreams.

When they get back to the car Sorrel is sitting in the back seat, smiling.

Ruben smiles back.

29

A New Year Begins
As It Means to Go On

"It's now or never," says Sorrel. She is standing on the foot of Celeste's bed, staring down at her, fully dressed and arms akimbo. "Either you tell her today or you forget about it. You can't keep waiting for the perfect moment. Trust me, it's never going to come."

Celeste opens one eye. It's still dark outside. "I know. I know," she mumbles. "But it's Saturday. I just want to stay in bed a little longer." And promptly rolls over so that her face is in her pillow.

It was generally agreed that the Christmas concert was an unqualified success. The orchestra's half of the programme and the individual performances of the second segment all came in for praise, but so, too, did the set design and presentation. Even Mrs Snowbird, the principal, a woman who doles out approval as if it's a dwindling resource, said it met professional standards. Indeed, only one person who attended the concert failed to show any enthusiasm for the event, and that one person is Lilah Redwing. How could she be expected to enjoy an evening that brought her nothing but embarrassment and humiliation? That's what she'd like to know. How? There she sat, surrounded by people she's known most of her life – by friends, colleagues, and people to and for whom she has sold houses (some of them very important people) – while the father of her children swanned to the front of the auditorium with "that man", flaunting their relationship in front of the entire town. She's convinced that even people who had never known Tylor when he was a respected professional and family man, knew who he was. Who else could it be? After all she's done for Celeste, this was the thanks she got. She's grateful they don't live under a fascist regime or Celeste would probably turn her into the secret police. And then, to add a whole lot of insult to a truckload of injury, and ignoring all of the distress and unhappiness she'd caused, Celeste abandoned Lilah and Astra to go off with her father and his whatever-you-want-to-call-him. To eat pizza! That's what betraying her mother and sister is worth to her, two slices of pepperoni with extra cheese and a diet Coke.

Since that fateful night, the relationship between Celeste and her mother has made the Cold War between the United States and the Soviet Union look like a Utopian dream. There are no walls and no spies or double agents, no shoe banging or aerial reconnaissance, no stockpiling of nuclear weapons or unveiled threats, but there has been a certain amount of sabotage (on Lilah's part) and a definite coolness and difficulty with negotiations. Celeste's mother doesn't yell and scream as Sorrel's mother did, and she doesn't go in for long sub-Arctic silences like Officer Gwinnet or (also like Officer Gwinnet) sudden outbursts of violence. Lilah Redwing is a tactician who would make Machiavelli proud. She acts as if nothing is wrong. She is sweet and pleasant, she smiles and smiles as if she is lit from within, she answers questions, she gives instructions, she asks Celeste about her day – but she does it all from very far away, as if she is no more than an image on a computer screen. The virtual mother; you can see her and hear her, but you can't get close.

Which is why Celeste hasn't managed to tell Lilah what she's decided about college. Celeste has been waiting for a good time, but because Lilah is avoiding her while pretending not to, there hasn't been even a not-so-bad time, let alone a good one. Lilah is always distracted. Always busy. Always in a hurry. Always on her way somewhere, or not yet returned.

"Don't go back to sleep!" orders Sorrel. "Get up. You have to be waiting for her or she'll be out of the house before you get your mouth open."

Celeste groans, but rolls onto her back. "Maybe I should wait till tonight. You know, when she's relaxed."

"Maybe you should wait till you're ninety and she's dead," says Sorrel.

Celeste sits alone in the kitchen for over an hour, silently rehearsing what she's going to say. She appreciates all her mother's done for her. She knows her mother only wants what's best for her. The last thing Celeste wants is to hurt her mother or cause her any pain. And she has applied to all the colleges her mother suggested – the ones near home, the ones with sound teaching programmes – but she's also applied to one college in the city. Her first choice; her only choice, really. The plan, made during the Christmas visit – suggested by Tylor before Celeste could bring it up, and seconded by Jake – is that she will live with them and try to get somewhere with her music while she studies, though not for a teaching degree. Maybe music history; something that actually interests her.

Celeste is on her tenth run-through of this speech when Lilah bustles in, her handbag and briefcase in one hand, her shoes in the other and her coat over her arm, muttering to herself about being late and so much to do and not enough hours in the day.

Celeste looks up with a smile. "Morning, Mom," she

says as Lilah bustles past her. "There's coffee and toast. And I made you a lunch."

"Thank you, darling." Her mother doesn't look at her, but drops her shoes on the floor, her bags on the table and her coat over the back of a chair, then goes over to the counter to pour herself a coffee.

"I could make you eggs, if you want," says Celeste. If she were a servant she'd be bowing and scraping. "It wouldn't be any trouble."

"No time, darling." Her mother sits down, taking her tablet from her handbag, and flips it open. "Busy day. Appointments until the afternoon."

"When will you be home? You want me to fix supper?"

"Not for me, darling." Lilah lifts her mug with one hand and swipes the screen with the other. "I have a date."

"A date?" Celeste fails at not sounding surprised; Lilah hasn't had a date since the Autumn. "You mean with a man?"

Her mother looks in her general direction. Slyly. "Well, it wouldn't be with a woman, would it?"

"I didn't mean... I only meant—"

"I won't be back till late," says Lilah, her eyes on the screen once more.

"Oh, right." Celeste lifts her own mug, then puts it down again. "It was just that I thought maybe you'd have some time to talk. You know, you're always so busy. And I have been trying—"

"Oh, I know you're trying, Celeste," Lilah says to her tablet, "but I don't suppose you can help it."

As if someone called her, Sorrel appears in the chair across from Celeste. "She's pushing your buttons," says Sorrel. "Don't let her do that. Make her talk to you now."

Celeste clears her throat. "Mom, I really need to talk to you. I know you're still mad at me about the concert and everything—"

"I'm not mad, darling." She shuts the Notepad and puts it back in her bag. "Why should I be mad? After all, no matter how badly he treated and hurt you, he is your father. There's nothing that can change that." More's the pity. "I understand that." She finishes her drink and gets to her feet. "And you are almost eighteen. You can make your own decisions. You don't have to worry about my feelings or what I think."

"And she doesn't have to worry about yours. Only, like always, she's not going to listen to your decisions." Sorrel leans towards Celeste. "Don't let her get away."

"Mom." Celeste stands up, too. "Just ten minutes. I really—"

"Not now." Lilah puts on her coat. "I absolutely have to go. My life is important, too, you know. Not everything's about you." She picks up her briefcase and handbag. "You have a nice day."

Celeste stands there, watching her mother walk out of the room, without once having looked at Celeste.

"Maybe it's a good thing I got hit by that stupid car." Sorrel is speaking very loudly. "Because if you can't even tell your mother you want to live with your dad and go to college somewhere she doesn't approve of how on earth would you ever have told her about us?"

"I would have." Celeste is whispering. "I would have."

"No you wouldn't. And you're never going to make anything of your music, either. You're going to go to college forty miles away and come home every weekend and become a teacher and marry some guy your mother thinks is a good provider and have two kids whose lives you can make as miserable as yours – and a whole lot of regrets."

Her mother's car is just clearing the garage when Celeste comes tearing out of the house, yelling at her to stop. Surprised, Lilah does stop.

Sorrel stands on the porch. Looking pleased.

30

You Can't Please All of the People
All of the Time – and Then There
Are People You Can Never Please

These days, Orlando is always in a hurry. He races from school to dance class, or from school to basketball practice, or from dance class to basketball practice, or from basketball practice to drama club, or from drama club to basketball practice on what is an enormous virtual hamster wheel. He is so busy and so tense that if he saw a large, neon sign that said RELAX it would take him several minutes to work out what it means. And even when he'd worked it out, he would be as likely to relate it to himself as he would an ad for horseshoes. Horseshoes? What does that have to do with me? I don't have a horse.

Besides always being in a hurry, Orlando is, of course, almost always late for one thing or another. Tonight he's going to be so late getting home that he'll miss the curfew his father has imposed during basketball season. There'll be no burning the candle at both ends for Orlando, not after what happened when his brother tried it. And

291

especially not when one of the ends is a career in professional basketball.

Coach Mena held Orlando after practice this afternoon for a little coach-to-player talk. "I know where your body is," said Coach Mena, "but I'm not so sure about your mind. I thought you'd pulled yourself together. You were playing like you used to for a while. But since Christmas you play like you're blindfolded and wearing boxing gloves. If you keep on like this…"

Since Christmas Orlando keeps thinking about people living the wrong life. Sorrel should have been able to love whomever she wanted. Her mother should have done what she wanted. His mother should have married a man who wouldn't treat her like his housekeeper. His father should have followed his dreams himself or found different ones.

Coach Mena shook his head. Less with sadness than disappointment and disgust. "You seem distracted. Not focused. Like you don't even care. Like tonight? Tonight balls were flying by you like birds."

Which was a massive exaggeration; it was one ball, one bird. Orlando mumbled something about school pressures. "It's senior year, you know? There's a lot going on."

Sounding disturbingly like Officer Gwinnet, the coach said that basketball is just as important as school, making it clear that he meant more important. Orlando promised to try harder. Again.

"Where have I heard that before?" asked the unsmiling Mena.

"Much, much harder," said Orlando.

As if that wasn't enough, Stella Brood held him after the run-through this evening for a little director-to-cast-member talk, too. "I know you can't give us all the time you'd like," said Stella Brood, "but I want you to know that you're doing a fantastic job. We're all really impressed." Besides being in the chorus line he's been given a small speaking part as well. "Now, I don't want to put you under any extra pressure, but I was hoping you'd agree to be Malik's understudy." As a reward for being so fantastic. "I've been dithering about it because I don't think anyone else is really up to it." Orlando pointed out that Malik, the lead, doesn't really dance. "That's why I'm not making him your understudy," said Stella Brood. "I know it's a lot to ask, but I do hope you'll take it. This would be good practice for you. Sort of cutting your teeth. It'd be a shame to waste your obvious talent." Talent. He has obvious talent. When did that happen? Orlando knew he should say no. It was crazy; he was already stretched so far it was a miracle he hadn't snapped, but, of course, he didn't want to say no. He doesn't want to waste his talent either, not now that he knows he has it. And he's enjoying being in the play; a lot more than he's ever enjoyed basketball. He said he'd do his best. "That's all I wanted to hear," said Stella Brood. Orlando can only hope that Malik doesn't drop out before opening night.

Of all the things to be late for, home is the least forgiving. If his father could install a time clock, he would. Orlando isn't that worried tonight because there's a bug doing the rounds of the station, so his father's been working overtime this week. Nonetheless, as a precautionary measure, he drives home as fast as he can without risking a ticket. Where his father's concerned, he can't be too careful. Unfortunately, it seems that he hasn't been careful enough. Either that or his father's colleagues have all had miraculous recoveries and he hasn't had to take on any extra hours. Officer Gwinnet is at the front door before Orlando gets out of the car.

"You know what time it is, boy?" His father steps off the porch like a policeman who knows you were speeding and isn't going to take any guff. "Where the hell have you been?"

Orlando freezes, standing on the ground but holding on to the car door. "I had practice."

"Don't give me that crap. Practice was over hours ago."

"I was hanging out with some of the guys."

"Do I look like a vegetable patch that you think I need manure dumped on me?" bellows his father. His fists are clenched. "I talked to Mena. You didn't go anywhere with anyone. He kept you after. He kept you after because you've been messing up again. Lying to me and messing up! So where the hell have you been?"

Dancing the night away, where else?

This, however, is no time for jokes. With every word out of his mouth, his father takes another step towards him. *Thump. Thump. Thump.* Orlando can see his mother at the living-room window, curtain twitching, looking worried if not actually terrified.

Which makes two of them. It doesn't happen often, but his father has been known to throw a punch. Suzanne and Orlando have both walked into more than one wall over the years.

It's Sorrel who screams, "For Christ's sake, Orlando, get in the car!"

Officer Gwinnet is so surprised to see his son suddenly jump back into the driver's seat and slam the door shut that he stops in his tracks. "Where do you think you're going?" he shouts. "You come back here!"

But Orlando is already almost out of the driveway.

Sorrel, looking out of the rear window, watches Orlando's father recede and then turns around to face the road. "Phew. That was kind of scary. I really thought he was going to deck you."

Orlando, catching his breath, just grunts. He thought so, too.

Sorrel stretches out in the passenger seat. "And to think you were having such a good day."

"Was I?" Orlando's heart is galloping. It's amazing how quickly a good day can turn into a bad night. "I don't remember that right now."

"Well, you were. Okay, not with Mena. That was pretty bleak. But with Stella it was ace. You can't've forgotten that already. The way she praised you. All that stuff about not wasting your obvious talent. Didn't I tell you that you'd be good at acting?" Apparently death does nothing to encourage modesty. "I hope you remember who pushed you into this when you're a famous Broadway star."

"Like you give me any chance to forget you." He looks into the rear-view but his father isn't pursuing, blue light flashing. "And you know what, Sorrel? I'd really like to forget you. I'd like to forget about you the way I've forgotten the name of the kid who sat next to me in kindergarten. But instead you keep popping up all the time. Needling and niggling me. And making things worse. Like this. Now I'm really in trouble."

"In trouble for what? You didn't do anything, Orlando.

So one time you break this bogus curfew. Big mega deal. It's not like you were out drinking till three in the morning. It's not even midnight, so you're hardly late at all. He's just riled because you didn't do exactly what he wanted. For God's sake, you're eighteen – he can't keep you on a lead for ever. You have to start acting like an independent person sometime."

There are few things more guaranteed to cause anger than someone telling you the truth you don't want to hear.

"Christ. Why don't you leave me alone?" He slams his hands down on the wheel and hits the horn. "Look at me. You listened to your crazy mother and I listen to you. I'm going to have to go back." And face the wrath of Gwinnet.

"But not yet," says Sorrel. "Give him time to calm down."

"And what should I do instead? Drive around in circles all night? I don't even know where I'm going."

"Yes you do." She points through the windscreen. "You're going there."

He comes to a stop in front of Ruben's. The house is dark.

"He isn't in."

"Of course he's in. Except for school stuff he pretty much goes out less than a cloistered monk."

"Okay, maybe he's there. But you know he's not going to let me in. It's been like a year since I got through that door."

She sighs. Apparently he's being exasperating. "Then why did you come here?"

Because this is where he always came when things were bad.

"And anyway, you don't have anything to lose. The worst that happens is Ruben won't let you in and you go home and get a black eye."

What a choice.

Orlando climbs out of the car and walks up to the front door. He rings the bell. It doesn't work. He knocks. He knocks again.

"Keep your shirt on!" He hears Ruben coming from the kitchen. Sees him peer through the peephole.

"It's me. Orlando."

Ruben opens the door.

From somewhere behind him, Ruben's mother calls, "Who is it? Is that Orlando?"

"Yeah, it's Orlando," Ruben calls back.

"I had no place else to go," says Orlando.

Ruben steps aside. "Then you'd better come in."

Orlando glances over his shoulder as he steps into the house. Sorrel is still in the passenger seat, watching him. Making sure he goes inside. Not that she has to worry about that.

31

Death Changes Everything

~

June

The anniversary of Sorrel Groober's death is warm and sunny, a day that shines with life.

Ruben parks the car and walks down the tree-lined path that leads to Sorrel's grave without any hesitation. This route is another of the things he'll never forget. There's something about carrying a coffin that makes a lasting impression.

It's early – Ruben's on his way to work – so he's surprised to find that he isn't the first visitor of the morning. There is already a large and expensive bunch of flowers – similar to the one Sorrel was waving around the time he saw her in the cemetery outside Peakston – lying beside the headstone. He stands at the foot of the grave, smiling as he reads the inscription. It says neither: *After all we did for her, this is how she thanks us*, nor: *If we'd known this was going to happen we wouldn't have spent all that money on her teeth*, but: *Treasured Daughter and Sister, you will always be missed, always loved* – and beneath it: *Death is not the end.*

"Death is not the end," reads Ruben. If the last twelve months has taught him anything, it's that. He opens the bag he's carrying and takes out a framed print of the painting he did from the photo of them all at Sorrel's birthday last year. He leans the picture against its base. "I thought you should have a copy, too," he says, "but, you know, I didn't want to put it out in bad weather." In some ways he can't believe it's been a whole year; and in some ways he can't believe it's only been one. Everything's so different from the way it was. The lights are back on in the Rossi house, Sylvia is back to herself and planning an extensive author tour in the Autumn, and Ruben's using all the money he's saved to take a year off to travel, paintbox, brushes and pencils in his backpack. The only thing that hasn't changed, of course, is that Sorrel is still dead. "But never gone," says Ruben. And this time removes a single red rose from the bag, laying it on the top of the stone.

The only time she was in this cemetery, Celeste had been in such a state that she has to get directions to the site from the office, and even with map in hand gets so confused that it takes her nearly half an hour to find Sorrel's grave.

She sees immediately that she's not the only one to remember what day this is; people have been here before her. The picture could only have been brought by Ruben – she has the same one hanging on the wall of her room. She's not so sure about the rose or the elaborate bouquet.

"I just thought I'd stop by and say hi. You know. I'll be leaving for my dad's soon, so I might not get another chance for a while." Celeste has no flowers or pictures, but she has brought a gift. "I wrote you another song."

And without so much as looking around to make sure that she's alone, Celeste closes her eyes and begins to sing, her strong, clear voice mixing with the rustling of the leaves and the cries of the birds and the silence of the visitors at other graves who have stopped what they were doing to look up and listen.

Orlando arrives late in the afternoon with a dwarf lilac in a plastic pot, a bottle of water and a trowel. He wanted blossoms, but it's late for that. It was his mother who suggested he actually plant a small bush. "Then, whenever you come back to visit, it'll be there." Which wasn't a statement but a question: *You will come back to visit, won't you?* Of course he'll come back to visit his mother. Who, unlike his other parent, came to the Peakston Players' performance and beamed with happiness at the party afterwards; has given him money to help him get started on his new life and is still speaking to him. Who is proud of him and not enraged with disappointment. Suzanne thinks his father will come around – in time – but Orlando isn't going to hold his breath. If Bernard does, he does; if he doesn't, then that's his call. Orlando no longer intends to lead Bernard's life for him.

Orlando kneels in the grass. Remembering Sorrel and the scent of lilacs, remembering carrying the casket from the hearse, one foot after the other – but mainly remembering her. Thinking about having a future, he digs a hole beside *death is not the end*. When it's deep enough, he tips the tiny shrub from its pot, being careful not to cover any of the words, patting the earth down around it. Then he gets to his feet, brushing the soil from the knees of his jeans. "Sorrel Marlene Groober," he reads out loud. "Treasured Daughter and Sister." Then adds, "And friend."

Like Ruben and Celeste, Orlando stops and looks back as he leaves the grave, thinking he might see Sorrel sitting on her own headstone, waving goodbye. But he doesn't, of course.

The dead don't hang around once the job is done.